What the critics are saying…

"Dragon's Fire is hot, hot, hot! Tielle St. Clare has created a fantastic yet believable world of magic, might, love, passion and dragons. Her characters are real, her stories filled with adventure, humour and passion." ~ *Historical Romance Club*

"Dragon's Fire was nonstop sensuality and action. The story had a perfect pace to it, and revealed each portion of the story at just the right time…Dragon's Fire is right up there with all my favorite erotic romances." ~ *Dani Jacquel Just Erotic Romance Reviews*

"The exciting and erotic love scenes are among the best I have read. Ms. St. Clare weaves her tale through a land full of magic and dragons and brings you along for the ride…This is definitely a must read." ~ *Jennifer Brooks Coffee Time Romance*

Tielle St. Clare

Dragon's Fire

ELLORA'S CAVE
ROMANTICA PUBLISHING

An Ellora's Cave Romantica Publication

www.ellorascave.com

Dragon's Fire

ISBN #141995167X
ALL RIGHTS RESERVED.
Dragon's Fire Copyright© 2004 Tielle St. Clare
Edited by: Briana St. James
Cover art by: Syneca

Electronic book Publication: August, 2004
Trade paperback Publication: May, 2005

Excerpt from *Just One Night* Copyright © Tielle St. Clare, 2003

Warning:

The following material contains graphic sexual content meant for mature readers. *Dragon's Fire* has been rated *E-rotic* by a minimum of three independent reviewers.

Ellora's Cave Publishing offers three levels of Romantica™ reading entertainment: S (S-ensuous), E (E-rotic), and X (X-treme).

S-ensuous love scenes are explicit and leave nothing to the imagination.

E-rotic love scenes are explicit, leave nothing to the imagination, and are high in volume per the overall word count. In addition, some E-rated titles might contain fantasy material that some readers find objectionable, such as bondage, submission, same sex encounters, forced seductions, etc. E-rated titles are the most graphic titles we carry; it is common, for instance, for an author to use words such as "fucking", "cock", "pussy", etc., within their work of literature.

X-treme titles differ from E-rated titles only in plot premise and storyline execution. Unlike E-rated titles, stories designated with the letter X tend to contain controversial subject matter not for the faint of heart.

Also by Tielle St. Clare:

Close Quarters

Dragon's Kiss

Irish Enchantment

Just One Night

Simon's Bliss

Dragon's Fire

Prologue

Rainek couldn't contain his groan as her lips closed over his cock, taking him deep in her mouth. Flat on his back, he fought the urge to thrust upward. He held himself still, letting her move on him. The hot flicker of her tongue across his skin was like a lash of wet fire, making him impossibly harder.

He gripped the sheets beneath him and held on. He would let her have control—let her take him. She pulled her mouth away and he almost screamed in frustration. But she moved, sliding up his body until she straddled his hips.

"I want you to come inside me," she whispered, the sound dancing across his skin. Her hands slid up his sides, caressing his chest and stomach. "I want to ride you long and hard."

"Yes. Do it," he growled through clenched teeth.

She only laughed. A deep seductive sound that hardened his cock even further. But, thank the Gods, she continued her upward movement until her pussy was immediately above his erection. Her tiny hand circled the thick shaft and she placed it against her opening. Her hot feminine moisture seduced him, called to him. Despite his best intentions, he thrust up, needing to be inside her.

Her teasing laughter taunted him as she lifted herself away.

She hesitated, just long enough to make him fear she would leave him, then with a smile that said she knew his thoughts, she sank down—accepting his hard cock into her body. Her soft, satisfied groan poured across his skin like liquid silk. The tight grip of her cunt was like nothing Rainek had ever imagined. She was perfect. She held him so tightly inside her body—hot and wet and his.

She quickly established a torturous rhythm, riding him slowly as if she wanted to savor each inch of his shaft. Her firm, tight breasts bounced each time she sank down. He wanted to reach up and touch her but his hands were bound to the bed, chained by the vision above him.

"Yes," she hissed pushing down hard until he was seated fully inside her again. She ground her hips in a circle.

"That's it, baby. Ride me." He groaned the desperate instruction.

Her pace increased. Long slow penetration faded in favor of quick shallow thrusts. She moaned and flipped her hair back. Gammon, he wanted to see her face. Wanted to see her eyes when she climaxed. Her rapid breath filled the room. He could feel her, she was close. The sweet vibrations of her cunt around his cock told him she was coming.

"Come inside me, Rainek. Fill me."

The plea was too seductive to resist and Rainek threw back his head and released his seed.

He jerked awake as he came—his cum spilling through his fingers onto the bed sheets. He continued to stroke his cock, feeling the last bit of pleasure fade. As he fell back against his blankets he listened to the soft chuckle echoing in his head. "Damn it, Denith."

You needed release, the sanctimonious voice responded.

"I need a wife. If you'd get off your ass and pick one, we'd both be a lot happier." He dragged himself out of bed and went to the basin to clean up. This had been happening on an increasingly frequent basis. The damned dragon that shared his mind—and sometimes his body—was taunting him with vague images of his future wife. The woman was never the same—her body changed from night to night and her face was hidden from his view. But that didn't stop the desire.

When I find the right woman for us, I'll know. Until then, you'll have to be satisfied with your nighttime releases.

But that was the problem. He wasn't satisfied. His body was eased but the physical release did little to calm the ache inside him. He wanted *her*—the one woman who would please both him and Denith.

"Do you have a specific kind of woman you're looking for?" he asked softly. He didn't need to speak out loud for Denith to hear him but he usually did so. It made it seem a little more real. Though he'd lived with it all his life, he knew the rest of the world did not share thoughts with a dragon.

I'll know her when I find her.

Denith had been saying that since Rainek had hit puberty and started having distinctly sexual urges. Urges that Denith wouldn't let Rainek satisfy with any woman but the one the dragon chose as his mate. So, at the ripe age of thirty summers, Rainek remained a virgin. A reluctant, frustrated virgin at that.

He felt the desire of a young man—more so because of the highly sexed dragon that filled part of his personality—but there was no relief. He'd tried—he'd kept company with beautiful women hoping that Denith would select one. He'd even gotten so far as to crawl into bed with one or two of them. He'd been excited, his partners had been aroused but his body wouldn't respond. If it weren't for the nightly hard-ons and morning climaxes, he would think there was something wrong with him. Something besides having a dragon in his head. But no, his problems were the dragon's fault.

"You know, my father was able to fuck women before he met my mother." The complaint sounded petulant and childish but Rainek was getting desperate. If he didn't fuck someone soon he was going to explode.

That is because Nekane had not come into being and had not yet selected Lorran as his mate. Patience.

Rainek shook his head. He was being told to be patient by a dragon. No one in the world would believe it. Dragons were known and feared as wild dangerous creatures. And Denith was telling him to be patient.

Sounds in the courtyard drew his attention away from the irritating thoughts. Bright laughter told him his sister Kayla was awake, and being as the sun was up, that meant Bren was out of bed. His older brother was always up before the sun and worked well beyond its setting.

Rainek shrugged into his clothes and went out to meet his siblings. They were closer than most brothers and sister. The reality that each of them was half-dragon had set them apart from other children so they'd clung to each other.

"Morning," he greeted, his voice still groggy from sleep. As he'd predicted Bren was there—dressed and tidy, looking remarkably tense for this early in the day.

Kayla looked up and smiled as Rainek entered the courtyard. Her bright yellow gown was already smudged with dirt and what appeared to be traces of jasmine jelly.

"You're up early," Bren said, offering Rainek a roll.

"I want to get an early start," he said, not wanting to reveal that Denith had been playing with his dreams again. Though if anyone could understand, it would be his brother and sister.

"I can't believe you accepted the invitation." Kayla flipped her hair back over her shoulder. She looked young and delicate but there was no mistaking the intelligence in her eyes. Or the worry.

"Why not? Queen Leika has six daughters. She wants to marry them off. All I'm going to do is meet them." And hope that one of them would satisfy the dragon inside him.

"And what happens if Denith doesn't choose one? How do you explain to the queen that it isn't her daughters you're rejecting? It's just that *your dragon* doesn't see any of them as a fit mate." She nudged Bren with her elbow. "Tell him, Bren. This could cause a rift between the two realms."

"I agree, Kayla, but Rainek has chosen to do this so we can't stop him."

Rainek had a vague notion of waving his arms above his head to alert them he was still in the garden.

"I think we'll just have to rely on Rainek's diplomacy to—" He looked pointedly at his younger brother. "—Not piss off the queen if he doesn't choose a wife from amongst her daughters."

"Ha! Rainek? Diplomacy?"

"Very funny," Rainek finally interrupted. "I'll be fine." He tilted his head and stared at his sister. There were more concerns than his inability to be polite. "Why are you so worried?"

"They're witches. All of them."

"We're not exactly normal. And I can't believe you listen to those rumors. Besides, I doubt they'll go after a prince. They want an alliance between our nations."

"They want alliances with all the nations," Bren pointed out. He tracked the political situations in the Seven Kingdoms. Though not officially part of the Seven Kingdoms and not members of the King's Council, the Matriarchy of Thearna was a powerful entity. The sisters of the queen were married to kings and princes throughout the lands and they wielded great power. She obviously intended to do the same with her daughters.

"I'll be fine. Are you sure you don't want to go with me?" Rainek asked Bren. "Maybe not one of the princesses, but it *is* a nation of women. Surely Tynan could find a mate amongst them."

Bren's lips curved downward. "It wouldn't matter if he did."

Kayla glared over Bren's head to Rainek and Rainek mentally kicked his own ass. He'd forgotten for a moment. Bren hadn't waited for the dragon to select a woman. He'd met a sweet, gentle lady and instantly lost his heart. Unfortunately, Tynan hadn't agreed. Since then, Bren hadn't been interested in finding a mate.

"When do you leave?" Kayla asked, obviously trying to turn the subject away.

"I'm packed and ready to go."

Bren reached beneath his leather vest. Rainek felt a sharp prick against his breastbone and the room around him wavered for a moment. Kayla straightened in her chair and Rainek knew she'd been jolted by the same sensation. They both looked at their older brother "I just wanted to be sure you were both wearing yours," Bren said.

Rainek placed his hand on the medallion that hung around his neck. Kayla's chain draped down into the top of her gown. The medallion was shaped — not surprisingly — like a dragon. All three children had them and wore them without fail. Between the dragons' mental powers and a bit of Nekane's blood, a wizard had been able to make the amulets, allowing the siblings to connect with each over other long distances.

"I just want to make sure you're safe."

Rainek nodded. Bren was a bit stuffy, but very protective. "How many men are you taking?" he asked.

"Just a small guard. Five."

"Are you sure that's enough? Once you cross into the Matriarchy lands, you're in their world."

Rainek laughed and shook his head. "You, too? You don't seriously believe the rumors that they kidnap male travelers and use them as sex slaves, do you? Not even the Matriarchy would dare that."

"You know the rumors about our family?" Bren asked, calmly sipping his coffee. Rainek nodded. "Most of them are true."

"Well, I'll be fine," he said with the arrogance of a man raised to rule. "I'm a Prince of Xicanth and I'm half-dragon. Denith won't let anything happen to me."

Chapter One

The pounding inside Rainek's head and the furious ache of his arms warned him before he'd even opened his eyes that he'd placed too much confidence in Denith's ability—or perhaps willingness—to keep him out of trouble. The dim torchlight pierced his brain as he let his eyelids drift open. By all the Hells, what had happened to him?

Keeping his movements small, to limit jarring his throbbing head, he looked around. Well, it was easy to see why his shoulders hurt. Metal bands surrounded his wrists and stretched his arms up and toward the opposing walls. The bands were connected with thick chains, each link the size of a man's palm and attached to a huge bolt lodged in the stone walls. He tugged experimentally. The metal cut into his skin but he made no impact on the chain. Not that he'd expected much. When one was using chains to hold a prisoner, one didn't use soft metal.

Prisoner. The thought startled Rainek for a moment. He was someone's prisoner. But whose? And why would someone kidnap him? By the Hells, who would have the bollocks to kidnap him? His family was rich but demanding a ransom would only bring the wrath of a dragon down on their heads. Few were willing to risk that for some gold.

A faint brush of cool air drew his attention downward. He was naked, stripped of his clothes and bound to the wall at four points. A quick glance over his shoulder revealed open space behind him as well. He was situated in the center of the room, almost as if he was being put on display.

Rainek jerked again on the chains and growled when they held firm.

Patience, the dragon preached to him.

"Bite me," Rainek said without rancor and flipped his arm to wrap his hand around a link. Using all his strength, he pulled and lifted himself off the floor. Matching cuffs on his ankles stopped him from rising more than an inch. With a growl, he relaxed down.

Damn it, what good was it being part dragon if the dragon decided to sleep when they were attacked?

I can't be awake all the time. Then you would be awake all the time.

Rainek decided to ignore that bit of dragon logic. He didn't need the damned beast inside his head to point out the truth. They'd been ambushed and captured while they slept. Surely a dragon should have sensed that coming.

If you'd let me take my form, I might have.

Rainek closed his eyes. Denith, of course, would bring that up. During the four-day journey toward the Matriarchy lands, Rainek hadn't let Denith take his corporeal form when they'd stopped for the night. The men in his guard found it unnerving to have a dragon in their midst. Most of the guard knew that Rainek was part dragon but actually seeing that fact manifest itself was a completely different situation. Having a fifty-foot dragon share their campfire was more than most were willing to endure.

It did no good to explain that the dragon had no interest in anyone in the guard, as long as they didn't attack Rainek. Being as there were no females in his guard and the dragon viewed none of the men as potential mates, there was little chance that Denith would even notice them.

Speaking of which, what had happened to his men? He was alone in the chamber. They'd set up camp just beyond the Matriarch boundaries. Two more days of hard riding would have brought them to the queen's stronghold.

Rainek stared at the chamber. It seemed unlikely that he'd been carried as far as the queen's castle. Despite the headache, it didn't feel like he'd been asleep for two days. The last memory he had was the tent above him disappearing and a sharp pain in his leg.

And then waking, naked and chained to the walls of a large chamber. The dim light would have allowed a normal human to see little beyond the small space in front of him but the dragon senses were sharper. Only the darkest shadows were hidden from him. Counters and tables stretched along the walls with implements and herbs he didn't want to know the use of scattered on every available surface.

Whatever this chamber was used for, it didn't look pleasant.

"I don't suppose you'd be willing to take your form now and break these chains," he asked Denith.

Denith was silent and Rainek could almost hear the beast considering the option.

Unwise, the dragon answered. *If the bands around your wrists don't break, I could end up footless when I appear. Let us wait to see who has captured us.*

Rainek yanked on the chains even though he knew the futility of it. It gave him a way to expend his frustration. He didn't care who in the Hells had captured him. He just wanted to be free.

Patience.

"Stop saying that," Rainek snarled. The only reaction was the quiet chuckle of the dragon. One of these days he was going to get his revenge on the beast.

Rainek glanced down at his chest. Along with his clothes, his amulet was gone. There was no way to contact his family. But he knew his brother. Bren was methodical and a bit dull, but he was protective of the family. If Rainek didn't check in within a few days, Bren would come after him.

The long, slow creak of a door opening shattered the irritated silence in Rainek's head. Maybe this was his answer. He took a deep breath and stood tall on his bare feet. Whoever it was, he wasn't going to be slumped over and weak when they entered.

He snapped his head toward the door, keeping his face impassive, hoping to catch his captors unaware.

He worked hard to hide the surprise as a woman strolled into the dungeon—her tall form decorated by a deep blue gown. Her breasts were small but pushed high and almost free from the tight bodice. The hint of a rosy nipple was visible. Crystalline black hair hung just to her chin, smooth and straight and with a soft swing to it as she walked toward him. Confidence and power emanated from her.

Whispers of movement behind her distracted Rainek. He looked beyond her, curious to see who else had entered the room. He could see the bottom inches of a gray gown but the rest of the person was hidden in blackness. The first woman before him stepped forward, obviously wanting his attention.

It took his mind a moment to catch up but reality slammed into him with a sick masculine shame—he'd been captured by a woman!

The idea grated on his warrior sensibilities but logic helped him push his annoyance aside and deal with the situation.

He'd been kidnapped by the Matriarchy. Maybe the rumors were true.

Rainek felt his lips pull up in a reluctant smile. They would be disappointed when they learned the truth about him. He was the wrong man to use for a sex slave.

He flattened his mouth and intensified his stare, ready to face his captors. "By the Dark Hells, what do you think you're doing?" he demanded. He gave a definitive tug on the chains to show he was serious. "Where are my men?"

"Don't worry about your guard. They're safe and enjoying our hospitality as we speak." The woman's voice was low and seductive, compelling his attention with the darkness that lingered beneath her words. "We rarely find it necessary to hurt those who come to us. They find much pleasure while they are here. As will you." The husky tone and intriguing words lured him, tempting him to forget for a moment that he was chained to a stone wall.

She walked closer. She was quite beautiful—her body long and thin, with high breasts and barely curved hips. Bright blue eyes glittered beneath long lashes as she boldly observed his naked form. Her perusal lingered long on his crotch.

Rainek shifted uncomfortably beneath her stare. He wasn't embarrassed about his body, but the blatant inspection was intrusive. It was as if she was shopping for a stud.

She raised her clear blue gaze to his and he could see the approval in her eyes. He turned his head away breaking the visual lock she had on him. He didn't mind bold women—had actually found them intriguing—but this went beyond boldness to aggression.

"I'm Princess Merena, sixth daughter of Queen Leika. Welcome."

The announcement sent a shock through his system. Why would a princess of the realm kidnap him? Particularly when the purpose of his visit was to meet the princesses and possibly select a wife.

"I can't say it's been a pleasure so far, Princess."

"I'll change that," she said in the same husky voice. "You'll never want to leave." The sensual way she spoke was compelling and distracting.

But annoying after awhile.

Denith's assessment broke the alluring spell and made Rainek smile. The princess seemed to realize he was laughing at her. She drew back a step and her eyes lost some of their twinkle.

He decided it was time to go on the offensive. "Why have you brought me here?" he asked, standing tall in his chains.

"All will become clear later." She walked in front of him, her hips swaying gently.

Irritated with the vague answer, Rainek drew in a deep breath and glared at her. He didn't need a —

A foreign scent invaded his lungs — sweet, delicate, warm. *Delicious.*

Instantly, his cock hardened. Being naked there was no way to conceal it. His body knew what it wanted and it wanted whoever was creating that enticing fragrance. His shaft continued to fill and began to rise.

Unable to resist, he drew in another lungful and savored the distinctive perfume. It was her. He'd found her. His mate. Denith growled his approval and it was all Rainek could do not to shout his triumph. The irritating dragon had finally picked a woman.

A second smell battled with the one that called to him but Rainek pushed it aside. Nothing would distract him. After thirty summers, Denith had finally chosen a woman. A mate!

I can have sex! Rainek could barely contain his joy and focused his attention on the woman in front of him, really looking at her. Princess Merena's beauty was legendary in all Seven Kingdoms. And the legends hadn't exaggerated. Of all the queen's daughters, Merena's was the name spoken with longing and passion. Her beauty, her sensuality had lured kings and princes to plead for her hand. She'd turned down more proposals than stars in the sky, or so rumor would have it. Looking at her now, Rainek could well believe it.

She was stunning — tall, elegant and almost no ass. If given his due, he would have requested a little more in the butt area — something to hold onto as he drove in deep — but she would do. He hoped she was up for some hard fucking because he didn't think he could hold back. Her cool beauty didn't give him the impression of someone who liked to burn up the sheets but he had to believe Denith knew what he was doing.

His cock pushed higher, eager for her pussy. She smiled and Rainek felt a strange shiver of concern down his spine. The icy color of her eyes didn't change.

"Hmmm, well, this is a nice start," she said, her voice triumphant and mocking, all hint of courtesy gone.

She stepped away and Rainek crushed the growl that started at the base of his throat. She walked to the shadows and spoke. Seconds later the delicious scent was gone.

Mine. Bring her back.

Don't worry, Rainek whispered to the dragon. *She's returning.* The heavy metal door swung shut as the princess walked back into the light. Her hips swung provocatively as she strolled forward. The predatory gleam in her eye made Rainek grip the chains even tighter but he held still. This was his mate. She was beautiful and a princess. Focusing on those aspects, he still found himself tensing as she stepped close.

Without prelude, she reached out and wrapped her hand around his rapidly expanding cock and…his shaft began to wilt.

He searched his head for Denith's presence, demanding answers without words. This wasn't supposed to happen. Not now. How could he fuck her if his cock didn't stay hard?

Not her, Denith replied though his tone implied he was as confused as Rainek was.

Merena looked at her hand and his limp cock, then stared up into Rainek's eyes. Determination and fury lit the beautiful blue, but no lust.

This was the wrong woman. Where was his mate?

* * * * *

Tiana pulled the door shut behind her as she exited the training chamber. No doubt Merena would be inside for a long time. There was no reason for Tiana to stay.

But she couldn't make herself walk away.

She sagged against the wall and stared at the door.

It could be hours before Merena decided she was done with the prince. If the rapid rise of his cock was any indication, he was ready and eager and Merena would put that to good use.

Before Merena had kicked her out, Tiana had had the chance to see just a hint of his full size. He'd been long and thick—and still growing. Heat rushed through her skin and her sex began to weep. She shifted, rolling her ass against the wall, trying to combat the image of the sexy, defiant prince.

Gammon, she was in for an uncomfortable night of unfulfilling dreams. With visions of the handsome prince dancing through her sleep, she would awaken tomorrow morning, aching and in need of release. Tiana rapped her fingers against the stone. When Merena had arrived two days ago, she'd brought with her a dozen sex slaves. Maybe there was one Tiana could use for the night.

She tugged on the suddenly too tight bodice of her gown. The sharp movement scraped her nipples, making them tighten and press against the rough wool material. She'd dressed in a hurry, hoping to catch Merena before she entered the training chamber and had forgotten to put on her chemise. Tiana dropped her head against the wall and blew out her breath in a long, forceful sigh. Despite her hopes, there would be no relief tonight. She would wait here until Merena was gone and then she would make sure the prince was taken care of.

She didn't share Merena's confidence that Prince Rainek of Xicanth would be her willing slave by morning. Merena had a reputation for easily seducing men but the prince seemed tougher than the usual selection. Of course, that didn't explain why he'd gone from defiant to an almost full erection in seconds.

Either way, Merena would have fun with him. The prince was lovely—all strong muscles and tight, sharp angles. Wide shoulders that tapered down to a slim—but not too slim—waist. Thick, powerful thighs that gave the impression he could spend hours pumping between a woman's legs. Reacting to the picture in her head, Tiana widened her stance.

And even better, he was very well hung.

As soon as the thought came to her head, Tiana rejected it. It didn't matter how handsome, muscular or even hung the captive was. The fact was, he belonged to Merena. She'd captured him.

Tiana grimaced. *And she brought him to my home.* The Keep was a remote outpost of the Matriarchy, usually used as a base camp for hunting crews or traveling members of the Ruling Family.

Or for hiding very special captives.

Tiana slapped her open palm against the stone beside her hips. Unable to ask the guard to assist in his capture, for fear that the queen would discover what she'd done, Merena had drafted Tiana into helping. While Merena cast a heavy sleep spell over his guard, Tiana had dealt with Prince Rainek. His eyes had widened for one moment as the tent had been ripped away into dust. She'd jabbed the needle into his thigh and he'd slept peacefully throughout the journey to the Keep. He hadn't moved or woken, even when they'd stripped him and chained him into position inside the training chamber.

Her pussy contracted at the memory of peeling his sturdy, functional leathers from his body. She'd discovered hard, lean muscle beneath—a warrior's body. This was no soft prince who commanded without involving himself. The calluses on his hands indicated he spent long hours working with a sword.

His guard had been well organized and efficient but Merena's magic was strong. After they'd collected the prince, they'd sent the guards out for his men. Even now, they were being washed and fed and would be taken into the slave chambers for use.

As Merena had said, the men wouldn't be harmed—as long as they cooperated. Tiana sighed and made a mental note to check on them as well when she was done for the evening. Somehow she knew Prince Rainek would not be happy if his guard was abused.

She wandered a few feet down the hall before turning around and going back. She knew she should leave but she had nowhere else to go. She didn't fit in with the women who existed in court or those who made up the guard the Matriarchy based out of the Keep. It was difficult to bond with others. There were too many chances that her secret would be exposed. That left her alone most of the time. And sometimes lonely.

As the annoyingly self-pitying words sunk in, the image of Rainek came to her—naked and eager. He could ease her loneliness. The fantasy built in her mind, creaming her already needy sex. How lovely it would be. She closed her eyes and let the unlikely image filter through her thoughts.

Her—kneeling above him—taking his cock into her pussy. Giving him a slow sensual ride. He felt so good, so thick. She wanted it to last but she needed to move faster. She placed her hands on his shoulders bracing herself for a long wild fuck. He growled his approval, the hot fire of his amber eyes gazing up at her. She dug her fingers into his shoulders and began to move. Her breasts rocked with each thrust. Rainek's hands were free and he reached up, taking her nipples between his fingers and pulling lightly, countering each penetration with an arousing stroke. The alternating sensations reverberated through her sex. The pressure built, until she thought she'd scream with the need to come. Just a little deeper, harder—

A door slammed open and Tiana spun around, facing the sound.

Fury lit Merena's face as she stalked out of the training chamber and into the corridor.

"What's wrong?" Tiana asked, stepping forward, slowing the furious princess. "What happened?" She'd seen Merena irritated, annoyed, even angry, but rarely did Merena allow the emotions to move all the way to rage.

"Nothing," Merena answered through tightly clenched teeth. Her eyes glinted with the hardness of diamonds. "Nothing happened."

She swirled away, the heavy silk of her gown creating a delicate slithering sound as she moved. Tiana stared first at the training chamber door and then at the princess stomping down the corridor. Curiosity sent her chasing after Merena.

When she finally caught up with her, Tiana fell into step.

"What happened?" she asked again, feeling bold because of her role in the prince's abduction. She was as much involved in this as Merena. "Did he hurt you?"

Merena stopped and turned on Tiana. It wasn't only fury that flickered in her eyes. It might have been described as hurt but Tiana was sure it was indignation. "A *man* could never hurt me," Princess Merena snarled. "He'll be begging to let me have him. Begging."

Tiana had no doubt that was true. She knew Merena's methods. They were powerful and convincing, if not quite ethical.

"I'll give him the night to think about what he *really* wants and tomorrow morning I will take my pleasure on him." The grim tone sounded far from pleasure but Tiana knew better than to comment. "Prepare him and clean him," she ordered. "And make sure that no one touches him. He gets no relief unless I give it to him, do you understand?"

Tiana nodded then realized what she was doing. "Wait. Me? You want me to take care of him?" An invisible band wrapped around her chest but she broke through it with a full breath. She was a member of the queen's household, not some slave maid. "Isn't there someone else who could do this? Someone more appropriate?" *Someone not so fascinated with his body?*

Merena's gaze changed with a variety of emotions—pity, amusement, perhaps even some sympathy—then her eyes hardened.

"The fewer who know he is here, the better. The queen will understand when I present her with my consort but until we are officially joined and I'm pregnant with his...child, I would like to keep the news of his presence between us. You understand, don't you?" She reached out and placed her hand on Tiana's forearm. "You, of all people, should understand what it's like to have a secret. A secret that could be damaging if the world found out about it."

Though the words were said with sympathy, Tiana heard the threat behind them. Merena would keep Tiana's secret if she kept hers.

A familiar pain roiled through her chest but Tiana crushed it as she had so many times before. There was nothing she could do. Merena knew the truth. Tiana took a deep breath and let the moist air flow into her body. Just the slow process of breathing gave her strength.

"I'll take care of him for you."

Merena smiled with a kind of smug triumph that made Tiana want to scream. Actually it made Tiana want to punch the pretty princess but that would be unwise. Merena wasn't merciful to those who crossed her. She liked having people in her power and because she knew Tiana's secret, Tiana would do what she was told.

As if Merena could see Tiana's thoughts, she laughed softly. "I'll return to him at first light. I'll expect him clean, oiled, and hard for me." Her low chuckle held a deep cruelty that made Tiana shudder with dread. Merena would break the prince's spirit to get what she wanted. "I know I can trust you, Tiana." Merena placed her soft fingers along Tiana's cheek and jaw. "Power comes from passion, after all." Tiana held herself stoic against Merena's taunts.

She was right, of course. Tiana was probably the most trustworthy person in the Keep. Add to that the fear that her secret would be exposed and Merena could be well assured that Tiana would keep her distance. With a final smile, Merena continued down the corridor. Her stride was no longer angry, as if teasing Tiana had improved the princess's mood.

Tiana's own irritation didn't stop the wedge of envy as she watched Merena walk away. The feminine sway of her hips—highlighted by the subtle shift of her skirts—attracted attention wherever Merena went, drawing the gazes of men and women alike.

With a sigh, Tiana pushed her hair away from her face and turned back toward the training chamber. The envy was only a momentary thing. She'd learned long ago that her strengths were organization and staying in the background to make sure the Keep ran smoothly. It was only on rare occasions did she find herself wishing for the confidence that Merena had. The confidence to approach a man and expect him to fall at her feet in lust.

The image made Tiana smile for the first time all evening. She couldn't imagine Prince Rainek on his knees before anyone. Particularly, not her.

She approached the chamber cautiously, first peeking around the corner of the open door. Rainek stood tall, glaring fiercely and pulling on the chains that held him bound to the walls. Tiana slipped inside, hiding in the shadows—watching him struggle against his bonds.

It took considerable strength not to lick her lips at the delicious banquet put before her. Thick solid muscles pulled across his chest and shoulders—powerful muscles used to hard work tapered down to an etched, rippling stomach.

His dark brown hair hung to his shoulders, growing matted with sweat as he fought against the manacles. His strong arms tensed—as if he was trying to rip the chains out of the stone. Tight creases delineated the muscles in his stomach, contracting with each pull of his shoulders.

The entire picture was one of strength—from the determination in his face to the power in his shoulders. And more. Even chained to a wall he exuded danger.

While she watched him she wondered how long the defiance would last. Somehow tonight, he'd managed to send Merena away without getting what she wanted. That wouldn't last long. Merena liked her men to cower before her and she'd broken others, leaving nothing behind but a shell, trained to follow her every order. There would be little left of the proud, powerful warrior when Merena finished with him. Sadness filled Tiana's chest at the loss. He didn't deserve this.

Her eyes dropped. The thick heavy length of his penis hung between his legs. Tiana couldn't resist staring at it for a moment and wondering what it would feel like, full and hard inside her, sliding deep as she rode him.

Unable to stop herself, she whimpered with the softest of breath.

"Who's there?"

Tiana mentally cursed herself for getting caught, but knew she was well hidden in the shadows. There was no way he could see her.

His eyes immediately found her in the dark.

"Come out," he commanded with an arrogant lift his chin. Though he was the one chained, Tiana followed his instruction, stepping into the light. A flicker of surprise wavered in his eyes. He'd obviously been expecting Merena or someone just like her.

The intent focus of his gaze made her hesitate.

"Who are you?" he asked, his voice dropping to a whisper.

"Uh, I'm Tiana. I've been assigned to, uh, take care of you." *Bathe you, clean you, touch you.* Guiding her thoughts away from that dangerous direction, she brushed her hands down the front of her skirts. Her palms seemed to be sweating. Strange. She had no reason to fear him. He couldn't reach her, couldn't harm her, but that didn't stop the slow roll of her stomach as she took another step forward.

Prince Rainek pulled himself up using the chains and leaned toward her as if he wanted to be nearer. He'd almost lifted himself off the floor.

Tiana waved her hands to gain his attention. "You can't break the chains and you'll just hurt yourself if you try."

His eyes widened and she felt the full weight of his stare. But he seemed to be looking into her, through her, beyond her — anywhere but at her.

She tried again. "Merena hexed the chains. They are unbreakable."

"Closer."

"What?" He didn't seem to be listening to her.

"Come closer."

She looked around the room. Was he even talking to her? Seeing no one else, she walked forward. Her legs trembled as she moved. She knew he couldn't get free but still, he radiated a power that Tiana felt deep in the core of her being. She didn't fear him; neither could she resist his command.

She drew to a stop two feet in front of him and waited. Nerves bounced inside her stomach.

"You!"

Tiana looked over her shoulder again. She was still alone, so she shrugged and answered. "Uh, yes."

"*Mine!*"

She shook her head. "Uh, no."

Chapter Two

"Mine!" he repeated.

Tiana jumped back at the guttural word breaking from his mouth. He was practically drooling.

She sighed softly. What a shame. He was beautiful but seemed incapable of using words with more than two syllables. *All the lovely ones were either crazy or stupid.* He tugged on the chains she'd just told him he couldn't break. *This one appeared to be both.*

Lust exploded in his eyes and his cock sprung forward as if reaching to her.

Gorgeous, crazy and horny.

And she was going to spend the night with him.

* * * * *

Rainek stared at the woman, *his* woman. His mate.

Yes. Mine. Denith struggled for freedom, making Rainek tear at the chains to get to her.

Patience, Rainek had the satisfaction of telling the dragon. *She's here. We'll have her.*

The dragon backed down but that didn't ease the steady throbbing in his groin. He had a feeling nothing would ease it except plunging into his mate's wet pussy. He took a deep breath and smelled her. The delightful scent of her sex—faint and sweet—reached him first, then the soft floral fragrance of her shampoo and the soap she used to wash her skin.

Delicious.

Rainek couldn't help but agree with the dragon's opinion. He could almost taste her. Wanted to taste her.

"Are you all right?"

He grimaced and nodded. He needed to keep Denith under control or she'd run screaming from the room. She seemed like a timid little thing. He couldn't quite imagine her, kneeling above him and riding his cock with lusty abandon but maybe there was something there he didn't see yet. There was definitely more warmth in her than in Merena. This woman's emotions echoed in her green eyes—her welcoming smile, her confusion.

"I'm fine," he assured her, trying to sound like a gentleman instead of raving beast who wanted to fuck her until she couldn't walk. Denith's approval of that plan—complete with mental pictures—distracted him until the dragon released the images and let Rainek return to the present. She was still staring at him--still curious but much more wary.

When she'd come into the room he'd been so stunned by her scent and the knowledge that his mate had returned that he hadn't truly looked at her. She looked nothing like the princess. Blonde riotous curls surrounded her head and tumbled down her back in a delightful state of disarray. She was short, almost dainty in appearance, until one looked at her breasts and her ass. She was well endowed in both locations. A perfect handful for his large hands. Instead of an elegant gown, she was dressed in a pale gray dress that had seen better days. It didn't worry him. He had plans to keep her naked for a long time.

Nor did it matter that his woman was a commoner, instead of the princess he'd come seeking. His family would accept her merely because Denith had done so.

She was not what he'd imagined when he'd taken the time to dream about his wife but it didn't matter. She was his.

She just didn't know it yet.

"What did you say your name was?" he asked. He'd been too distracted by her arrival to hear the words coming from her lips. He licked his own wondering what it would take to convince her to come to him.

"Tiana."

Denith stomped through his head telling him to grab her. Rainek did his best to ignore him. He'd heard the tales of his parents' "courtship" and the lengths Nekane had gone through to protect and claim his mate. Rainek had a little more control over Denith. The dragon had been in existence for all of Rainek's thirty summers. Rainek just had to convince him that this was the time for human interaction. The dragon would get his chance with her soon.

Denith howled his approval and Rainek felt his cock harden to the point of exploding. He was going to have to find a way out of these chains and into her pussy—soon. Neither he nor the dragon would accept any less.

Tiana stared up at the captive prince. He'd asked for her name and given no reaction that he'd even heard her. She waited, and after along moments, he seemed to regain control of himself. His eyes focused on her and she could tell he was actually seeing her. Whatever spasm had taken him was gone.

She flashed him a quick, supportive smile then turned away, intent on gathering a cloth and a bowl of warm water. She needed to get him cleaned up and ready for Merena's arrival. They hadn't exactly been rough with him when they'd captured him but some injuries were unavoidable. He was a large man and even with both her and Merena lifting him, they'd had to drag him most of the way to the cart. Who would have suspected him to be so large? And heavy? All that muscle weighed a ton.

As she filled the bowl with water, she surreptitiously glanced back at him. Speaking of big…her eyes returned to his cock. He'd been flaccid when she'd walked in but the beast had continued to swell and swell. Her pussy fluttered at the possibility and challenge of taking such a massive cock inside. A deep empty ache crept into her sex. This was the cock she wanted. She ground her teeth together and turned back to the sink. Maybe in exchange for taking care of the prince, Merena would allow her the use of a slave. There were others permanently assigned the castle but Tiana avoided using them whenever possible. She just found it strange to mount a man one night then ask him to chop wood the next day.

After bathing the prince she would definitely need something to ease her.

Brushing that thought away before it distracted her even more, she gathered what she needed and went back to his side. The weight of his penetrating stare had followed her every step. When she finally met his eyes, he grinned. As if he was just happy to look at her.

"Are you all right?" She'd never seen a captive react like this. They were frightened or angry—as he'd appeared to be when Merena had first walked in. Now, he seemed downright cheerful.

"I'm wonderful. I'm just so pleased to have found you."

She couldn't stop her wry smile. "Well, we sort of found you, if you'll recall."

She wheeled a cart beside him and placed the bowl and rags on top. It took all her strength not to groan as she viewed the task ahead. Forcing herself to move forward, she dipped a cloth into the water, wrung it out and slowly sank to her knees. The seductive, submissive position made her pussy contract with renewed need. Before him, on her knees, his cock prominent and hard and so close. Discovering that she was staring up at him and that her tongue was teasing the inside of her lips, she jerked her gaze to the floor. She had to keep herself distant and removed as she stroked—uh, scrubbed—the rag over his skin. Then realizing she'd delayed as long as she could, she began to wash his right ankle.

Dust smeared into muddy clumps. With a sigh, she added more water. The whole goal was to keep her attention on the job and the dirt—and not on the firm flesh beneath the grime.

It wasn't supposed to be a sensual experience. She was giving a captive a bath—a task usually reserved for the slave maids. But as the dirt faded and his skin appeared, tan and pink, she found her strokes growing longer, extending from his knee to his ankle and back up again. It would be so easy to lean forward and place her mouth on his—

She jerked back, not letting herself complete the thought. She needed something to distract her. Something to keep her mind occupied so it didn't wander into the fantasy of wrapping her lips around that massive—

She gulped and struggled to find her voice.

"What's your favorite color?" she asked. Drawing on her inner reserves, she looked up, deliberately staring past his erection and offering a cheerful smile toward the prince.

As if jolted out of his own sensual world, he blinked and then shook his head as if clearing away some wayward thought. Tiana swallowed deeply at the idea that he was having the same fantasies she was. Of course, if a woman were kneeling at a naked man's feet, he would most likely be having that fantasy.

She forced that depressing thought aside and watched his face for another moment. She could see him thinking, analyzing, wondering why she was asking, no doubt. She could hardly explain that she was asking inane questions to keep from laying him down, mounting him and riding him like this season's stallion. Her cheeks heated. She lowered her eyes and told herself to return to her task.

"I don't know that I've ever had one. What's yours?"

Amber, like the color of your eyes. She kept that response solely in her mind and shrugged. "Purple, I guess. It's such a royal color."

He chuckled softly as if her answer was part of a private joke but Tiana refused to look at his face to see his amusement.

"You like purple, do you? Excellent."

She squeezed the water from the cloth and began to wash his thigh. She tried to make her movements firm and efficient but it was difficult. The line of tight muscle called for long, drawn out strokes. She found herself retracing the already clean path down his lower leg then back up.

"I think my favorite color just became a deep luscious pink."

Knowing he watched her, feeling his gaze on her, she casually lifted her head as she reached up to sluice water down his thigh. "Why pink?"

"The color of your lips."

She saw his eyes dip down to her chest and somehow knew he was thinking about the color of her nipples. *Or that's what he wants you to think.*

Everything about him was sexual—from the heat in his eyes to his rampant cock, thick and straining for attention.

Tiana sat down on her heels, pressed her lips together and dropped the cloth into the bowl.

"Please stop." Though she tried to sound irritated, unshed tears welled up and immediately clogged her throat. She might not be the beauty that Merena was but that didn't mean she could be tricked by a few silky words. "I know what you're doing and it won't work. I might seem like an easy target but I'm not stupid." His eyes lost their humor and his lips parted as if he was going to speak. "You can't seduce me into letting you go, so just stop with the compliments and flirting. I'm your—" She grimaced. "Caretaker for the night. That's all."

There was a moment of stunned silence.

"I'm sorry," he said. He actually sounded contrite but then he'd *actually* sounded aroused so she knew Prince Rainek was a superior actor. "Truly, I meant no disrespect."

Sincerity overwhelmed his words and Tiana found her resolve weakening.

"It's of no matter," she said brushing it aside. She couldn't stop herself from glancing at his cock, then she jerked her gaze back to his knees. "Merena will return in the morning and then you can get what you want."

"Want you." His dark gravelly voice was harsh and sent a warning up her spine.

"Well, you can't have me," she dismissed. She wasn't a toy to be played with because he wanted to fuck now that he'd sent Merena away. "You belong to Merena."

"Mine!"

His voice changed with the cry and Tiana looked up. With a definite shake of her head, she spoke. "No. You belong to Merena."

Tension shot through his body in one sharp wave, starting at his strong shoulders and flowing down to the thin muscles of his feet. The chains creaked as he pulled on his restraints. Tiana jumped back, moving well out of his reach. The thick muscles of his shoulders contracted. His hands turned red then white with the exertion. A trickle of blood slipped from underneath the cuff around his wrist.

"Please, stop. You'll hurt yourself." She stepped closer. He whipped his head up and stared at her with eyes that were black. She'd never known black could be so hot. His lips were pulled back and his teeth clenched as if he was fighting to contain something inside him. "Please, is something wrong? Prince Rainek?" She placed her palm on his chest.

He froze as if stunned by her touch. She snapped her hand back, not wanting to cause him any more pain. As soon as her fingers left his skin, he began to fight again.

"No, wait, please, Your Highness. You'll hurt yourself." Needing at least a moment's respite, she returned her hand to his chest.

His struggles once again stopped, but he still stared with those fathomless eyes and the vicious tension in his body. Not knowing what else to do, she kept talking, calling his name and gently stroking her hand along his chest, soothing him. She continued the path down to his stomach, fascinated by the play of his muscles and the hot feel of his skin beneath hers. It would be so easy to reach down and curl her hand around his cock. Even as she thought it, she noticed her hand inching that direction. He was so thick. Her fingers wouldn't reach all the way around. It would take both hands to hold him.

With a quick intake of breath and quick glance at his face to see if he noticed her wanderings, she steered her touch upward. She winced at her own lecherous frame of mind. The man was obviously having some sort of attack and she was thinking of fondling him. The palms of her hands seemed to warm at the image. Whether the heat came from him or her she didn't know, but she kept up her long, calming strokes.

His eyes rolled back into his head, in pain or in ecstasy she couldn't tell. The change was slow but she sensed his transformation. After a long time, he began to breathe again and Tiana knew the mysterious crisis had passed. His shoulders shuddered as he drew in a long, cleansing breath. He flipped his hair back over his shoulder and looked at her with laughing, lust-filled eyes.

"Your hands are like liquid fire," he whispered.

Tiana drew her hands away, noting that he was right. Her hands burned with a strange heat. She surreptitiously looked at her palms as she stepped back. They didn't look any different. But a fever seemed to have invaded her palms as she'd touched him.

With a quick, bracing breath, she returned to her usually efficient self.

"Are you recovered?"

He laughed softly and a new kind of red flowed into his cheeks—he was blushing. Watching him, she realized he was cute. Not just handsome or powerful but there was a bit of shyness that made him cute.

"I've never been better."

The words came out seductive and sweet and Tiana felt them all inside her body. Her cheeks were warm but knew she couldn't let herself fall under whatever spell he was weaving. She had her obligations.

"I apologize for my...outburst," he said. The light in his eyes had changed again—glittering like gold beneath the sun. "I have certain reactions that I can't control."

That comment made her flick her gaze toward his crotch and the rampant cock still straining for relief. Rainek chuckled. "Yes, that as well."

* * * * *

As Tiana nodded and backed away, Rainek grimaced. Damn, they'd frightened her. It was strange that the dragon who had spent most of his existence preaching patience was unwilling to wait now that he'd found his little mate. Her casual announcement that he could not have her had sent Denith off in a rage. It had taken all of Rainek's strength to keep him contained.

Want mine.

And we'll get her, he assured the dragon. *But not if we frighten her and make her run from the room.*

Denith grumbled but let Rainek lead.

The slow gurgle of water drew his attention back to his woman. She rinsed the cloth and again dropped to her knees before him. It was all he could do not to punch his hips forward, to find a way to insert his cock between those deep pink lips.

Gritting his teeth against the sweet torture of her hands, hot and delicate against his skin, Rainek watched her. She seemed lost in her own thoughts as she ran the cloth up his legs, washing and rinsing. At times her touch seemed impersonal but at other moments he got the distinct impression she was washing and rewashing his skin just so she could touch him. Damn, he wanted her hands on him not that damned rag. When she'd stroked his chest, it had sent fires of need to his groin.

Denith quickly jumped into the game providing Rainek with a crisp, clear image of Tiana with both hands wrapped around Rainek's cock—stroking, squeezing. Rainek groaned.

The dragon's ability to visualize with precision made his fantasies hard to resist.

He silently assured Denith that he wanted the same thing but they needed to woo her. They couldn't just grab her and fuck her silly.

She's delicate and fragile, he warned the dragon.

Not that fragile, Denith replied and implanted an image of Rainek above Tiana, driving his cock time and again into her cunt. In his dream, she pushed back with equal force.

Rainek bit back a growl and focused his attention on his mate as she continued her task.

All the rumors he'd heard about the women of the Matriarchy was that they indulged in their sexual desires with abandon. That the men they kidnapped were used, shared and discarded when they no longer performed. But Tiana hadn't shown any of the sexual hunger he would have expected. She seemed intent on suppressing that side of her nature. He could see it humming below the surface. The brief flickers of lust in her eyes gave him hope that she would be willing to experience long hours beneath him. Or above him. He had no problem with her riding his cock.

Each successive image made his shaft rise. With the slightest touch, he would explode. He squeezed his lips together, resisting the urge to beg Tiana for that caress.

She finished with washing his legs, studiously avoiding his crotch, then rubbed a towel down each limb. Finally she stood, her lowered gaze locked firmly below his shoulders and above his waist. She obviously felt uncomfortable meeting his stare.

It was an intimate thing to bathe another in such a fashion. Trying to ease her fears, Rainek closed his eyes, giving her some distance between them. Through the bottom of his lashes, he watched her. Some of the tension faded from her shoulders.

She pulled her cart closer and began again her methodical cleansing, long slow swipes across his chest and stomach, down his arms. Occasionally he would feel her repeat the pattern, as if she was truly caressing him. These touches gave him hope she wasn't immune to him.

"Do you have a large family?" he asked, keeping his eyes mostly closed. She jerked at the sound of his voice. Rainek did his best to hide his smile.

"Uhm, yes. I have six sisters."

"No brothers?"

She shook her head. "No. Our women rarely birth boy children and when they do..." Her voice turned somber. "The child is either left to die or exiled to another land."

Rainek opened his eyes and stared at her. "What?! How can they do that?" He couldn't keep the appalled tone out of his voice.

"It is the way of the Matriarchy. A boy child might attempt to overtake the throne."

"You don't agree with this practice."

She shook her head. "I know it has to be that way but still...my mother birthed two boys. They were exiled at birth. I've always wondered what happened to them and what it would have been like to have brothers."

Wanting to push away her sorrow, he chuckled. "They are a torment and an irritation."

She responded as he hoped—with a soft smile. The pain faded from her eyes. "You have brothers, then?" She reached up, stretching long to wash his wrists. Her breasts pushed against the sturdy material of her gown. With the slightest movement, he could bend down and capture one delicious peak between his lips.

Resisting the temptation she placed so near his watering mouth, he went back to their conversation.

"One," he said. "And a sister. But my brother wasn't the tormentor." She looked over at him and he winked. "I was."

She laughed, dragging the cloth down his arm to his shoulder. "You admit it."

"Oh yes," he groaned, more in response to her dainty hands moving on his body—the way she stroked the sensitive skin beneath his arm. Denith rumbled in his head. Rainek clamped down the dragon, took a deep breath and went on to tell his story. "I went out of my way to torture my brother as often as I could. He's a bit stodgy, you have to understand. Has a plan for everything. I've never met a more controlled person. But he's a good man and a good brother. He'll make an excellent king."

"And your sister?"

"Oh, she'd make a lousy king." He was pleased when Tiana smiled at his teasing. "In truth, she's a terror, but being a girl, she gets away with a lot more than I do. My father dotes on her dreadfully." He went on to tell her stories, entertaining her as she washed him—anything to keep her close. Denith was much calmer with her beside him. She pushed up on her tiptoes to wash his neck. Rainek couldn't stop himself. He leaned down, drawing in the delicious scent of her hair, the sweet curve of her jawline. Her warm fragrance permeated his being. He could smell her—her arousal, her lust for him. He could almost taste her. Tiana paused and for a moment he thought she would turn and offer him her lips but instead she backed away. She dropped her rag in the bowl and gathered the rest of her bathing items.

Fearing she was going to leave, he twisted as she moved behind him.

"Just stand straight," she instructed, her voice breathless and soft. The heated scent that emanated from between her legs grew.

That was a good sign. She was becoming aroused by touching him.

But he didn't like that she'd moved behind him. He couldn't see her from there.

Tiana thanked her Goddesses that she was behind him now. He couldn't see her from there. The intensity of his stare weighed on her. He'd followed her command to stop flirting

41

with her but that hadn't lessened the impact of his attention. He'd still tracked her movements with hungry eyes and a predator's stare. She felt a like a rabbit within a hawk's sight.

She brought clean water and placed the bowl on the cart. He was amazing from the back as well. His tightly curved backside made her palms ache—not with the strange burning but with the temptation to reach out and squeeze.

With him unable to watch her, she could look her fill. She took the opportunity as it presented itself. It wasn't often she got to observe such a delightful male specimen. She did her best to remain distant and aloof but it was hard. His back was as powerful as his front. It made her want to mount his backside and rub her body all over him.

A whimper escaped her throat before she could stop it. By the Goddesses, he was beautiful.

"Are you all right, Tiana?"

"Of course, Your Highness. I just had something catch in my throat." *My heart.* She forced herself to return to her job, moving quickly. It was easier to be efficient when he wasn't staring at her. When she was finished, she dropped the cloth in the bowl and pushed her cart around to the front. The determined smile on her face made it difficult to speak but she did so.

"There. All done."

He shook his head. "Not quite, my lovely."

She instinctively pressed her hand to her stomach, trying to ease the ache that assaulted her at his words. "What do you mean?"

"There's one place left for you to wash." He glanced down then back up at her. Where before there had been teasing and laughter in his eyes—now there was a dare. "You wouldn't want Merena to think you'd shirked your duty, now would you?"

She pushed her shoulders back. "Of course not, Your Highness." He could see her swallow as if to gather her courage. She dipped the rag into the water. Rainek held his breath as she stepped forward and began to dribble water onto his lower stomach, down to his cock. Rainek couldn't stand it any more. He dropped his head back and released the groan that been building every time she touched him.

As if the sound emboldened her, she wrapped her cloth-covered hand around his shaft and began to stroke. He opened his eyes, unable to resist the sight of her touching him. Her teeth snagged her lower lip as she stared at his cock. The warmth he'd seen in her eyes ignited and flushed her cheeks pink. Heat flowed through the rag as if her hands radiated fire. She pumped down the length of his cock and it was more than he could take. Rainek pulled on the chains that held him and shouted as he spilled his seed into the cloth.

The room was silent, filled only with the sound of their ragged breaths. They both stood still absorbing the moment. Then slowly, she pulled back, wiping away his semen and reaching between his legs to wash his heavy sacs before walking away. Rainek sagged down in the chains. Coming had sapped the strength from his legs.

If that's what it feels like coming in her hand, how am I going to survive her cunt? he asked rhetorically.

The dragon answered anyway. *With pleasure.*

Tiana was gone for a long time but Rainek didn't protest. He needed a moment to recover. How embarrassing. It had taken barely two strokes of her hand — and a hand wrapped in cloth no less — to make him come. He was going to behave like a green lad when he actually got around to fucking her. Despite the reality that he was, in fact, new to sex, he hated the idea that she would believe him a man with no control.

Tiana returned, standing a few feet away, her eyes looking anywhere but him. He'd probably mortified her by coming in her hands. She crushed her skirt in her fingers. "Uhm, I need to lay you down so you'll be ready. For, uh, tomorrow. When Merena will return." Her cheeks turned a deep red, one that complimented the dusky pink of her lips.

"Tiana, about—"

She shook her head, silently commanding him to stop. Rainek ground his teeth together and did as she requested. He didn't want to embarrass her further.

"I'm going to lay you down now." She waved her hands toward the space between his legs and if he thought her cheeks couldn't get any redder, he was mistaken. "I, uh, need you to take a step out with each foot." Head down, she spun around and moved to the far wall. A series of levers stood out from the stone panel. Not understanding what was happening, he followed her instructions, curious about where this would lead.

"It's easiest if you can hold yourself upright as long as possible." With that cryptic advice, she pulled one of the levers downward.

And the ground below him disappeared. His feet still stood on stone but a gaping hole appeared between his legs as the floor fell away. He wrapped his hands around the chains at his wrists and pulled himself up. The loud grind of metal on metal drew his attention back to Tiana. A second lever was pulled down and a rush of air swirled around his ankles.

The empty space was slowly filled as a long flat surface rose from the black hole. The table that appeared was as wide as his legs could stretch.

"Don't fight the chains," she called, her voice was sympathetic and gave him strength. He wouldn't embarrass himself in front of his mate. At least he hoped he wouldn't. More noise reached him as the bands around his ankles pulled forward, lifting his feet from under him. He caught himself, holding the chains that bound his wrists as both sets of manacles raised him, until he was horizontal. Then slowly, he was lowered onto the long black table. The process took only moments. When it was over, he was stretched out, flat on his back. The chains slid down the walls until his arms were extended out to his sides. Another "ke-chunk" followed and supporting tables appeared giving him a place to rest his arms and shoulders. Overall, it wasn't terribly uncomfortable. As long as he had Tiana near him.

She walked to the tableside, pushing her messy blonde curls away from her face as she looked down at him. "I'm sorry about that. You'll get used to it. This room is designed to train slaves. The levers make it possible to have you upright for your training as well as on your back when your Mistress wants to mount you."

Rainek almost swallowed his tongue at her casual description. Then Denith repeated the image of Tiana kneeling over him, riding him, her cunt enveloping his cock time and time again.

"Yes."

A rush of disappointment filled Tiana's chest. The sensation surprised and confused her. What did it matter that he was excited about Merena returning to mount him? It just seemed a little strange after rejecting Merena tonight, why would he be pleased about her return tomorrow? *Particularly after he just came in your hand.* She ignored that snide thought, willing the memory away until later when she could enjoy it, replay it.

Maybe Rainek planned to play "hard to get" with Merena.

Tiana felt compelled to warn him it wouldn't work.

"About tomorrow," she said, staring down into his warm amber eyes, "when Merena returns, it's really best to just give her what she wants."

"Not Merena. Want you." His voice had returned to that same growling tone and the short clipped words that made her almost believe him when he said he wanted her.

Thankfully, logic came to her rescue and pointed out that the prince clearly thought she was a better target for sympathy and was still trying to convince her to release him.

She smiled tightly. "That's a lovely sentiment. Merena will return in the morning and she'll mount you." She shook her head. "I don't know what you did earlier to make her angry but she's quite powerful. Just give her what she wants and you'll save yourself a lot of pain."

Tiana patted his hand. She was ready to leave him for the night. She would return in the morning and stroke him to arousal. Not that he needed any help now. His cock was once again in a full, upright position.

She sighed. There was a lot she could do with a cock like that at her disposal. She swept her tongue along the inside of her lip.

"Let me taste you."

Tiana's head snapped up. "What?" It was almost as if he could hear her thoughts. She started to step away but stopped. He was so hard and ready. The ache in her sex moved deeper.

"I want to taste you," he repeated,

She felt her eyes widen. He couldn't really mean...

"A kiss to start. Is that too much to ask?"

A kiss wasn't that difficult. And he seemed so hungry for it. She started to lean forward, imagining his lips on hers, the slow subtle glide of his tongue in her mouth. She jerked herself away. He was doing it again.

"I told you. You can't seduce me into releasing you." She folded her arms under her breasts. "Merena would have the skin flayed off my back if I did so."

"I have no intention of begging for release." He smiled. "At least not release from these chains."

Tiana looked away. Somehow this man knew just how to tempt her, seduce her. She'd known he was dangerous when she first saw him. Now she knew why. He could tap into a woman's sensuality and play on her emotions.

Gathering her floundering courage, she returned her gaze to his. The open honesty in his stare melted her anger.

"I give you my word as a prince of Xicanth, as the son of King Kei, that I will not attempt to escape this night—that my words are not meant to seduce you into freeing me. I would like you to stay with me. I desire you. Let me touch you, taste you."

Some of the fear and suspicion faded with his vow. He seemed so sincere...and his cock was so hard. She licked her lips. She'd never taken a man's cock into her mouth. The possibility was intriguing.

"I guess a kiss would be all right." She glanced at his erection for a moment before smiling hesitantly toward his face. Rainek held himself tense, countering the dramatic strength of the dragon, waiting as she placed her hands on the table, next to his head and bent forward.

Her lips were soft and light. He remained still and let her brush her mouth over his, matching her caresses, slowly joining, opening. Denith shuddered with pleasure and Rainek could feel the dragon absorbing her taste, capturing it in his memory.

The delicate flicker of her tongue against his lips sent a new ache to his groin. Patience and restraint disappeared and Rainek pushed himself up, opening his mouth and plunging his tongue into her waiting lips. She didn't pull away as he feared. Instead, she met him, stroke for stroke, her hands slipping behind his head and holding him as they plundered each other's mouths. He nipped at her lower lip, needing something to release the pressure inside him. She groaned and the dainty rumble moved from her mouth into his.

He reached for her. The huge chains rattled, clashing with the quiet music of their mouths and heavy breaths.

Tiana jumped back. Her chest rose and fell in a frantic grab for more air. Rainek couldn't help but stare at her breasts. Though fully concealed in her buttoned up gown, the size and shape were obvious and would fit well in his large hands.

She placed her hand on her chest and took another step away. Denith growled and Rainek could feel the dragon rising.

"Please," he gasped.

Tiana glanced at the door as if to confirm it was closed, then looked back. Her eyes landed first on his cock then slid up to his face.

"Perhaps I can ease you."

Chapter Three

The heat in his eyes made her pussy clench with need even as she started to regret her offer. She wasn't supposed to do this. Merena had given direct orders for him to have no relief tonight but she couldn't leave him like this.

Tiana glanced at the herbs and potions on the counter. Merena had obviously given him some sort of aphrodisiac. There was no other way to explain how he could have returned to full hardness moments after he'd come.

A quick recovery with the intensity of his need could only mean one potion — *reconi* juice.

She silently cursed the princess. Despite the fact that it was illegal to use *reconi* juice on anyone except contracted pleasure slaves, Merena had been known to administer it to the men she'd captured.

It was a common drink for the women of the Matriarchy. In addition to acting as a way to prevent pregnancies, it gave them a light buzz and increased their sexual needs. For men, the reaction was more definite and painful. The aphrodisiac made a male hard, filling the cock until the man was pleading for release. The pain wouldn't retreat until he was allowed to climax over and over again. It sometimes took hours to ease the sexual need.

Tiana snatched her lower lip between her teeth and stared at the beautiful man before her. Could she really do it? It would be so simple. But there would be consequences. Still, it wasn't fair to leave him bound and hard all night. Tiana could give him the release he needed and then surely by morning his cock would become hard again at Merena's touch. It was hours before Merena would return. She'd said "first light" but Tiana knew that Merena had never seen the dawn—not even for a man like Rainek.

Unconsciously, Tiana smoothed her hand down his chest. She could well imagine rising early to take her pleasure with Rainek—or staying up until dawn arrived. Staying on him...all night long.

She pressed her lips together to crush a groan. The desperate ache in her sex seemed to be reflected in her hands—the strange, tingling heat had returned. Her hips swayed in an unconscious motion to match the growing need between her legs.

With a quick shake of her head to align her scattered thoughts, she made her decision. She couldn't take her pleasure on him but she wouldn't leave him like this either.

"Let me help you," she whispered in the quiet of the room. The words slipped from her soul with only the sound of her ragged breath to accompany them.

Slowly, her fingertips skimmed across his stomach, reveling in the tight muscles and smooth silk of his skin. The sweet freedom of touching him distracted her for a moment and she let her hands retrace their path until the draw of his formidable cock became too much to resist. After a moment's hesitation, she inched her fingers forward, sliding them into the nest of hair that waited. The curly strands wound around her fingers, holding her as she brushed the base of his shaft. Rainek inhaled sharply.

She pulled her gaze away from the luscious sight of his hard cock and stared at his face. Rainek's eyes were squeezed shut, his hands curled into claws, stretching against unbreakable bonds. As if fighting to reach her.

His eyes popped open and he stared at her. The amber faded from his eyes and left behind hot black. The visual caress was as real as a physical one. It penetrated her cunt, making her wet and weakening her knees. No man had ever looked at her this way. As if he wanted only her, desired only her.

Almost silent voices warned that he didn't desire *her*—he would want any woman who would fuck him. Merena had done this to him, and in the morning, Merena would have him.

A foreign defiance Tiana had never felt before bubbled up in her chest.

But I have him tonight, she thought.

Tiana left the sweet tangle of his hair and smoothed the flat of her fingers up the length of his cock. It was such a simple caress but so powerful. Rainek punched his hips up and he groaned with sharp sensation. Though tempted to wrap her fingers around the thick shaft, she pulled away and considered the situation.

She could have stroked him again to climax but she wanted more. Something deeper and more satisfying—without actually allowing him access to her sex. She was willing to defy Merena to some extent but actually mounting another woman's captive was tantamount to treason. Tiana stared at Rainek's cock and felt her lips open slightly. She knew some men found pleasure from a woman's mouth but she'd never actually attempted it. Few women in the Matriarchy even spoke of the practice. Men were designed to please *them*—not the other way around—and the thought of putting her mouth on his cock should have revolted her. Instead, she was fascinated. How would it feel against her tongue?

The thought gave her the inspiration to make her decision.

"I've seen others do this, though I've never done it myself." Before she could let herself rethink the insanity of her actions, she climbed up onto the table to give herself a better angle. His legs were spread, constrained by the bands around his ankles. She straddled one massive thigh and stared at the fierce cock before her. "Let me know if I hurt you, or do something wrong," she whispered. She hated this feeling of insecurity, this uncertainty about how to proceed but the desire to feel that thick rod between her lips drove her on.

She closed her eyes for a moment and tried to picture the female servants using their mouths on the captives, arousing them so that one of the ruling class could take her pleasure. But all she could remember was the moaning and masculine pleas for more.

Relying on instinct, she placed her hands beside his hips and lowered her mouth to the thick shaft. Her tongue slipped from between her teeth and with a short, dainty lick, she stroked the underside of the thick head. The hiss of air being drawn in through clenched teeth made her look up. She didn't want to hurt him. She wanted to ease him. To please him.

Heat exploded in his eyes and encouraged her to continue. She leaned further down, placed her tongue flat against his rod, and slowly drew upward. This time she didn't pull back when he tensed. She pressed her mouth against him feeling his warmth and life pulse beneath her lips. It was amazing—this lovely smooth flesh so solid and strong. So fragile. She lost herself in the sensation, learning him, discovering the sensitive spot at the base that made him groan. She tested his pleasure with long strokes and quick, kitten-like flutters. His thigh muscles tightened beneath her hand and she wanted to smile. He wanted more. So did she. She wrapped her fingers around his shaft and pushed the thick head between her lips.

"Yes, Tiana, honey, suck it, please."

With her mouth still covering the first few inches, she brushed her tongue along the underside and watched his chest arch up. Power surged into her sex.

Goddesses, she wanted to mount him. Knowing that was impossible, she would give him pleasure. She opened her lips a little wider and sank down. The thick rod filled her mouth almost choking her as she swallowed as much of him as she could.

"Tiana!" His cry was punctuated with a tiny pump of his hips. She relaxed her throat and accepted more cock. Then she began to move, pulling up and down, discovering a rhythm that made Rainek moan. Shivers of pleasure went down her own spine as she sucked on him, loving the glide of his shaft between her lips. Guided by the steady roll of his hips, she pumped faster, concentrating on that sweet spot at the base of the head.

"Honey, I'm about to come." He twisted his hips like he wanted to pull away, but she wouldn't let him. She wanted to enjoy all of him. She grabbed his hips, letting her fingers tease the curve of his backside, holding him in place. Her fingernails dug into his flesh with just a tiny bite as she kept up her frantic pace, feeling like she was on the verge of her own release.

"Tiana!" He exploded into her mouth. She gulped, letting his cum flow down her throat. She waited until each pulse had passed, then she pulled back, licking her way up his cock, lapping at the remaining drops.

Something completely sexual burgeoned within her. She lifted her eyes. His gaze was waiting for her. The vibrant power of his stare made her draw back. She licked her lips tasting him still on her mouth. Lust screamed through his body like a lightning bolt. And she was in control of his pleasure. Her mouth curled into a slow smile. Knowing he watched, she placed a dainty kiss on the tip of his cock. It was then that she realized he was still hard. Merena must have overdosed him.

Tiana looked at the hopeful eager glint in his eyes and couldn't resist another swipe of her tongue. She watched his eyes flutter shut and felt the delicious tremors weave through his body. He belonged to her. Hers to pleasure. And to tease. The drive to make him come faded and she began to play her mouth along his shaft, learning and lingering. Making him growl and loving every time he moaned her name. Warmth flared in her palms and she slipped her hand between his legs, cupping the heavy sacs that hung down. She lingered, stroking his bollocks, trying to capture them in her mouth.

"Tiana, honey, let me have you."

Her pussy, already dripping, swelled with need. Unconsciously she rolled her hips, needing something to ease the wild ache between her thighs but it was impossible. Giving him release was bad enough but taking him inside her body—Merena would never forgive that.

She slipped her hand down, pressing at the vee of her legs, hoping for some relief, but she'd never been good at giving herself release. Her fingers never found the right touch. It always left her aching for the full feeling of a cock inside her.

Her sex quivered in anticipation but Tiana clamped down on the sensation. She couldn't have him. She drew in a deep breath and focused on his cock. She would bring him to climax one more time and then she would leave.

"Turn around."

Dazed and lost in her own sensual world, Rainek's gentle command barely penetrated her mind. She opened her mouth and sucked his cock back inside, letting him stroke the inside of her mouth and bump up against her throat.

"Damn it, honey, please, turn around. Let me have your cunt."

His demand seemed to reach her that time. She lifted her head and Rainek felt his entire body tense.

Her lips were red and full and she had no idea how sexual she looked. His vague fantasies of his future mate sucking his cock had been obliterated by the exotic reality of her mouth. She knew just how to lick him, to bring him to the hottest arousal he'd ever imagined. Somehow the dragon had known, she was perfect for him. Confusion flicked across her face. She'd been fully consumed with sucking his cock and seemed to find his call an unwelcome distraction.

"Come over me so I can taste you, too." He kept his voice soft. Between his need to fuck her and the dragon's desire to rip the chains from the walls and claim her as his own, Rainek was surprised he was as coherent as he was.

Her breath brushed against his cock sending waves of too soft pleasure into his groin. He wanted her to suck on him again. Stuffing his cock into her sweet mouth had filled his dreams but other needs clawed at him as well. He didn't want to frighten her but the desire to taste her overwhelmed him. He needed to feel the sweet fluid of her pussy on his tongue. Denith needed it.

"Let me taste your cunt," he said again. This time, he could tell she heard him. Her eyes cleared and she straightened. She sat back on her heels, the rough woolen skirts hiding the sweet pussy he wanted to claim.

"I shouldn't," she said, shaking her head. "I—"

"Let me have you. Now."

The low gravelly demand was not the sweet seduction that most women would have wanted. She tensed and Rainek grabbed the chains, anticipating Denith's response if she refused.

Instead of moving away, she pushed up high on her knees and drew her skirts above her waist. Her hands trembled as she pulled the material up, baring her softly rounded thighs.

Rainek stared, not wanting to miss any part of her, hungry for his first glimpse of her delicious sex. Denith was almost panting with his need to taste her. He tried to soothe the dragon with the thought that soon she would be open to him, but the dragon's patience was at an end. She chewed on her lower lip for one long moment, then she began to move, crawling up his body. Every soft whisper of her skin on his—even the brush of her gown—was a teasing torment. Soon, very soon, he vowed, he would feel all of her against him, and feel his cock inside her.

The seductive perfume flowing from between her legs intensified as she moved closer. He could sense her hesitation but also felt her arousal. She wanted this. She teetered on the edge of the table.

"Come over my mouth," he instructed. "Let me taste you." An exquisite shudder flowed through her body. He was already anticipating her flavor. She was close. He almost had her. Need ripped through him as she stared down at him—her gaze focused on his lips. He could see her thoughts at work— imagining about how his mouth would feel against her skin. Almost reluctantly, she dragged her eyes away and skimmed down his body as if she couldn't decide which she wanted more—his mouth or his cock. "Turn around and you can have both." She flinched as if surprised that he'd read her mind. Then the idea seemed to take hold and she grinned. Moving slowly, no doubt to keep herself from falling off the table, she turned herself around until she was facing his feet, lifted one knee and swung it over his head. Darkness surrounded him for a moment as her skirts hung down, covering his head. He heard her muffled laugh and the heavy material was lifted away. She leaned forward and flashed him a shy smile.

Rainek grinned back. His little mate wasn't as delicate as he'd first thought.

He reached for her, forgetting for a moment that his hands were bound. "Sink down."

The soft flesh of her inner thighs settled around his head and her scent permeated his being. Denith howled his pleasure and Rainek stretched up, meeting her as she came to him, flicking his tongue softly against her sex, savoring the warm, musky flavor of her pussy. She gasped at the first touch and squirmed, sinking lower, giving him full access.

Rainek groaned. She was delicious—wet and hot. Open for his feasting. His desire to slowly learn her flesh was obscured by the dragon's desperate need to taste her, to make her come. He trailed his mouth down the length of her slit, sampling her flavor, promising himself more. Lifting his head, he placed his lips over her clit and began to suck. Her gasp turned into a yelp and Rainek couldn't stop his smile. He would bring her so much pleasure.

Tiana felt her eyes burn as she stared blankly into space. Whatever he was doing to her was creating the most amazing sensations in her sex. She'd had climaxes before—small, minor releases of pressure, but the buildup inside her pussy was already greater than anything she'd felt before. She'd climbed onto this table to give him release, now he was pleasuring her. And it was as if this was a pleasure for him as well.

Rainek kept on, steadily pulling on her clit. She closed her eyes and let the feeling spiral higher and higher. He hummed softly as he sucked on her. The tiny vibrations made her breath lock in her chest. He didn't relent—continuing the strong, steady pulls of his mouth. He seemed desperate for her climax and she couldn't resist. With a clear, sharp spike, the tension that had built inside her pussy shattered.

Tiana gasped and dropped forward, catching herself on the table. Her dress fell down, once again covering Rainek's head. That was fine. She wasn't sure she could face him just yet.

Clarity returned as her heart rate slowed and she realized she was truly kneeling above a captive, offering her open sex to his mouth. Even with no one else in the room, she felt herself blush. Not that this was an uncommon event. Even the table she knelt on was designed for this activity, crafted with two indents beside the raised headrest—perfect for a woman to kneel above a man and have him lick her pussy without strain on her knees or his neck. Tiana had known others who'd used this feature but she'd never found herself in this position. It was too intimate to have a man's face between her legs, but somehow tonight, it felt right. It felt necessary.

"More." Even through the curtain of her gown, she heard the demand and realized that when she'd climaxed she'd pulled away from him. She gathered the ends of her skirt up—not wanting him to suffocate—and, taking a deep breath, she slowly lowered herself until she could almost feel him. The sensation was still so new but now she knew the pleasure that was possible. There was no way she could resist it.

He began again, slower this time, as if his need had been eased when hers had. A long slow lick of his tongue moved along the inside folds of her pussy. Her breath caught at the back of her throat. The touch was so light that she was sure she'd imagined it. He repeated the gentle motion, deeper and longer. Her cream slipped out of her passage, leaving behind a trail of warmth. He gathered it onto his tongue.

Delicious.

Tiana heard the word in her mind and quietly breathed out her agreement. "Yes." She shimmied her hips, lowering further until he had complete and full access to her sex. His tongue fluttered over her flesh in light strokes.

She snapped her teeth together and tried to fight the pleasure. This was almost worse than the intense sucking on her clit. The rise to release was slower but the fall would be greater. Heat flowed through her sex — each lick, each caress a new fiery sensation — that spiraled out of her pussy and seemed to find a home in her palms. The burning had returned, hotter and stronger. The delicate caresses slowly faded and he began to work on her clit, circling the tight bundle before sucking on it.

Tiana felt her eyes roll to the back of her skull. She grunted and arched her hips, offering him more, giving him whatever access he wanted. He sucked and pulled and drew on the sensitive points until the sensations were too much, too strong to be contained in such a small area.

Her hips rolled without her command, seeking a deeper connection, wanting that deeper touch. He thrust his tongue into her passage and Tiana cried out. The release was sharp and wild — a new kind of heat filling her body, starting in her core and spreading into her limbs. Her elbows wobbled with the weight of holding her body. Gasping for desperately needed air, she waited, listening to her heart slow as the pleasure faded, drifting like smoke on a still night. Tiana opened her eyes, not having realized she'd closed them.

His thick cock stretched long before her, reaching up toward his stomach — toward her — as if begging for her attention. The desire to take him again in her mouth and drive him to climax crept up on her. Once more. She would allow herself to take him into her mouth once more.

And one more climax of her own.

Rainek didn't stop. He trailed his tongue from her clit to her passage, dipping the tip of his tongue into the tight opening. Tiana whimpered and returned the favor, placing her mouth over as much of his shaft as she could and sliding up until she could capture the head between her lips.

His groan rumbled through her pussy. She drew two inches of cock into her mouth and sucked lightly, focusing her attention on the very tip. Rainek pumped his tongue in and out of her cunt, flicking the hard tip against her inside walls. The delicious sensation distracted her but she wouldn't be denied.

She wanted to reach for his cock, to stroke him and surround him with her fingers—knowing she could bring him pleasure that way—but she held back. The prince didn't have use of his hands. Instead, she sucked him deeper, sending him to the back of her throat with the force of her thrust. His hips punched up but his mouth never slowed.

He nibbled on her outer lips, alternating the subtle touches with hard presses into her pussy. He obviously doesn't need his hands, she thought.

The sharp, sudden rise of her own climax drew her attention from his cock. She sat up and ground her hips in slow circles, hoping to force him to give her what she needed. The definitive curve of his mouth against her skin alerted her to his sensual game. He'd lured her away from her prize. With renewed determination, she returned her attention to the hungry cock before her, again sucking him into her mouth, drawing him deep, returning to the same subtle pressure that had pushed him over the edge the last time. His muffled groan was followed by an all-out assault on her pussy—his tongue everywhere, stroking everything, never settling.

Tiana took him deeper and began to pump, quick pulses, sucking each time she drew back. She didn't know how long she worked on him—lost in the dual sensations of his cock in her mouth and his tongue in her pussy—but she felt his body contract as if he was fighting his release. She couldn't have that, not when her own body was screaming toward that goal. Determined that he would come first, she reached out and stroked the tip of her index finger across his skin—first on the inside of his thigh then down to his bollocks. Heat seemed to pour from her hands but she had no idea if he would feel it—or if it was only in her mind. His hips punched up as she swirled one fingertip around the twin sacs. She kept her touch light countering with her strong oral caresses, faster and deeper. His mouth left her cunt and his hips rolled now in sharp upward punches. His harsh breath spiked against her skin as she pushed him hard, driving him toward release.

A long, loud groan preceded the first burst of his seed, filling her mouth for the second time. She swallowed, accepting it as her due.

She only had a moment to savor her success before his mouth returned to her sex. There was no teasing. He latched his mouth around her clit and began to suck. Her body, primed by his strong tonguing, vibrated and exploded, sending the pleasure to the ends of her fingers. She pushed up on her hands, let her head fall back and released a groan that sounded suspiciously like a howl. Her hips continued to pump, rubbing against his tongue, his mouth, as she strained for more. And more was there. Another climax followed quickly on the second. As that one faded, she sank down, collapsing on top of him, her breath coming in heavy bellows.

Face down, her cheek resting on his hip, she tried to restore her mind's command of her body. Finally, her heartbeat slowed, her breathing eased. And then, it began again. His mouth moved across her sex—soothing and sensual at the same time. She had a feeling she was in for a long night.

With barely enough strength to lift her head, she looked at her hands. The pain was incredible—as if she'd placed her palms against a hot stovetop. She imagined a wisp of smoke floating away as she stared.

More. Let me have more.

The pleading voice inside her head demanded her attention. And an answer. "Yes," she sighed.

* * * * *

Sobbing, Tiana sagged forward. "You have to stop. Please." She'd lost track of time — could barely remember her own name, though she remembered his. She'd screamed it enough times through the night.

She couldn't take any more. Heat and fire seared her veins with each orgasm. But Rainek didn't stop. The tip of his tongue slipped back into her pussy, massaging the inside edge until she thought she would explode — again. No, it couldn't happen. It was too much. No body could contain that much pleasure.

Finding a strength she didn't know she possessed, she pushed on up on her knees and flung herself off the table. In an inelegant dismount, she tumbled to the ground and landed sprawled on her back. A low, thoroughly disgruntled growl echoed through the chamber. Glass jars on the far counter shook with the vibrations. Tiana stared up at the table. Had Rainek made that sound? *How* had he made that sound?

She gasped in four shallow breaths before she even tried to stand. And then found her legs too weak to hold her. The muscles quivered as she gripped the edge of the training table and pulled herself upright. She leaned forward, and her nipples brushed against his thigh sending another wave of pleasure into her pussy. She'd lost her dress at some point. There was a vague memory of frustration as it kept getting in her way and then her ripping it off so she could feel her breasts brush against his skin. Her hair hung long and wild around her shoulders, falling in a tangled mass around her face. She swept it back and stared at the man who'd spent the last several hours with his face between her legs. The glint of her sex juices shone around his mouth.

"More," he demanded.

She shook her head. He might want more but she couldn't take it. Her body was about to collapse.

And her hands. The pain had grown worse with each passing hour. She curled her fingers into her palms and felt the heat bounce across her skin. Something was wrong with her but she didn't know what. Only that it had something to do with

Prince Rainek. This strange fever had begun when he'd arrived and begun licking her. Her knees wobbled and she straightened her elbows to hold herself up.

"Merena will—" She looked at his cock. He was hard again. Still. She'd sucked him off twice and he'd come beneath her hand twice more. Most men would have been beyond satisfied or at least on the verge of tiring. She cleared her throat, finding it difficult to speak with the images of the night still playing in her head. "Merena will be here in a short while."

"Want you. Only you." He licked his lips. "Delicious. Mine."

The words were like a lightning bolt into her sex. There was no doubting that he believed them. There was no way to fake the lust that crystallized his gaze.

Tiana turned away, resisting the temptation, knowing she couldn't bear to see the desire in his eyes. It seemed so real, so desperate.

The chains rattled and she knew he reached for her but she didn't look back. It was too risky. Her body shook with the weakness of extended pleasure but his was still strong. She glanced at the high, narrow windows. The sun was just lighting the sky and Merena would no doubt arrive soon to claim her prize.

"Merena will be here soon and you must let her...let her fuck you." It was like she was nailing her own hands to a wall but she kept on with the casual comments. "She'll expect you hard and ready for her." Tiana listened to the soft rumblings beyond the chamber walls. The household staff was waking and preparing for the day.

"Only you."

The determination in his voice drew her gaze back to him. He watched her with the same hot eyes that had lured her the first time. The chains that held him bound were pulled taut. He wanted her.

She shook her mind from the insipid thoughts. He was drugged. He had to be. He would fuck anyone. *Lick anyone.* But it was strange. She'd never heard of *reconi* juice doing that to a slave. It was designed to make them hard, make them want to fuck. But make them want to lick pussy? It didn't seem right, but there was no other explanation.

More.

Tiana heard the word distant and foreign. A sound no human could have made. She looked down at Rainek. His black eyes stared back. She'd never seen eyes that changed colors so dramatically before. His alternated between amber and black—always hot, always watching her.

The first rays of light slipped in the window and created golden slashes on the floor. It was time for her to leave.

Tiana found the crumpled pile of material that was her gown and pulled it back over her head. The rough wool didn't crush so there was not hint of the wrinkles from spending the night on the floor. She let the gown fall over her body. Her pussy—still damp from her own juices and Rainek's mouth—tingled as the soft material fluttered against her sex. Unable to stop herself, she raced her fingers downward, tripping across her sensitive flesh. She wanted more. She stared at the table. She wanted *that* cock—inside her.

"Tiana."

The desire that laced his voice sent a shock of pain into her cunt. She needed more of him. Heat exploded in her hands. Turning her back to Rainek, she uncurled her fingers. Fire erupted from her skin.

Real fire.

Tiny flames burst from her palms and leapt a foot into the air.

Tiana screamed and snapped her hands shut.

Oh Goddesses, what was happening? There was only one explanation of what was happening and it couldn't be. It *couldn't* be happening.

"Tiana?" The rattle of chains accompanied Rainek's call. "Are you hurt?"

"I'm fine." She walked into the far corner of the room, mostly out of sight from the training table, and held her hands before her. This time she peeled back each finger separately, until her palms were open. No fire erupted. Tiana sighed. Maybe it was a one-time event. Or her imagination. She'd been imagining voices in her head all night — why not fire in her hands?

Fervently hoping it was her imagination — because the reality would be too frightful to think about — Tiana pumped fresh water into a bowl. She had to rewash certain parts of Prince Rainek before Merena arrived.

Before Merena arrived to fuck him.

Tiana's jaw began to ache and she realized she was clenching her teeth. With a self-disgusted sigh, she grabbed a cloth and plunged it into the water.

The water hissed and steam rose as her hands broke through the surface.

She stared at the bowl. This couldn't be happening. After all these years it wasn't possible.

The slow clunk of the door being unlocked froze her in time for one eternal moment. Merena obviously hadn't been joking when she'd said she would arrive at dawn.

Grabbing the water and the rag, Tiana hurried to the table.

Rainek watched her with curious eyes. The lust was still there but it was tempered by concern.

"Are you all right?"

"Yes. Merena is here," she said quickly, as she wrapped her cloth-covered hand around his shaft, then stroked the insides of his thighs and stomach, until all traces of his seed were cleaned away. Her hands shook as she stroked his cock. She smoothed the rag between his legs, cupping again the firm sacs before moving on. His muscles tightened as she washed him.

"Please, don't mention last night. I—"

"Of course, I won't. Tiana—"

The door opened. Tiana willed herself not to tense. Not to react to the princess's arrival. Tiana glanced down at Rainek. A glimmer of moisture lingered around his mouth announcing her shame to any who saw it. She swiped the damp cloth across his cheeks clearing away any trace of her presence. Rainek lay still, enduring her ministrations while he watched her.

Hoping the high open windows kept the scent of hot sex and arousal from lingering in the room and alerting Merena to how they'd spent the night, Tiana dropped the cloth into the bowl and waited.

"Tiana? What are you doing here?"

She turned slowly and faced Merena. "I—uhm, finishing up with—with him." She nodded her head toward the table. The thick line of his cock was hard and strong. Good. Merena would be pleased.

"It took you all night to wash him?" The disbelief and mockery in Merena's question warned Tiana to be careful with her answer.

"Of course not. I simply thought that if he was tidied up this morning, he would be fresh for you." She offered a weak smile.

Merena pursed her lips together and slowly nodded. She looked around Tiana to Rainek's groin. "And he does look fresh, doesn't he?"

"Yes." It was a struggle for Tiana to keep the snippy tone out of her voice. And her hands were aching again. The momentary relief of plunging them in cold water hadn't lasted.

"Well, you can leave us now."

Tiana nodded and began to gather all the items she'd used to wash Rainek. Merena turned away, strolling toward the jars of herbs that lined the wall.

Tiana leaned down. "Remember what I said," she whispered.

"Don't want her."

"*Learn* to want her. She wants you and Merena always gets what she wants in the end. No matter how painful it is." She glanced back at the princess. Merena was combining liquids and powers. Slowly the potion turned a bright green. She was mixing a potent form of *reconi* juice. Tiana looked back at Rainek, and resisted the urge to brush his hair away from his face. She only had time for one more warning. He was a warrior. He would understand. "I know you're trained to fight to the death," she said. "But you'll lose this battle. It's easier for everyone if you give in now." She walked to the door. "Goodbye, Prince Rainek."

"Tiana!"

His shout shook the metal door but she ignored it and walked away. She sensed Merena's presence behind her as she stepped into the corridor.

"Tiana." The firm tone of Merena's voice made her stop. No one ignored the princess when she spoke in that manner. "Why would *my captive* be screaming your name?"

Heat smoldered in her palms and it was all Tiana could do to keep her fingers curled and hidden.

"You didn't give him release last night, did you?"

Tiana sighed. She didn't have time to deal with this. Her hands were on fire—*literally* on fire—and Merena was worried about whether her captive would be able to keep his erection. "Does it look like I did? He is hard and waiting, as you ordered." Anger gave her courage and she turned away. "I have to go."

She didn't look back, knowing that Merena watched her walk away.

Tiana turned the corner and collapsed against the wall. Her heart felt like a lump of rock in her chest and her palms burned with the fires of every level of the Hells but she forced herself to straighten and return to her own rooms. Rainek belonged to Merena now and there was nothing she could do except live on the memories.

* * * * *

Rainek/Denith stared as Tiana walked away.

Gone?! Mine gone?

The scream vibrated through his skull like his brain was bouncing against the bone. This was the first time he'd ever heard Denith use the barbaric panicked scream of a dragon about to lose its mate. Nekane was known for it. Denith had always been almost philosophical about the situation. For a dragon.

But now that he'd met her, tasted her, he wasn't going to let her escape him. Rainek felt the rise of the dragon's fury and there was nothing he could do to contain it. Without his command, he felt his shoulders tighten and his hands wrap around the heavy chains.

She'll be back, Rainek promised silently.

Want her now. Mine!

We'll get her back. You're going to rip my arms out of the sockets. The dragon hesitated for a moment.

The door creaked open and Merena strolled back into the room, her hips swinging in a low seductive manner. She approached the table with a suspicious glint in her eyes then boldly stared at his cock.

"Very nice," she murmured.

Denith rumbled.

Let me get us through this, Rainek silently asked Denith.

The dragon growled his disapproval.

Once we get rid of her, we can go after Tiana.

The promise settled the dragon and Rainek felt his shoulders ease. Denith relied on the smell of a person to learn their character. Rainek took a deep breath, gathering her scent by instinct.

A pungent floral smell clogged his nose. Denith rejected it out of hand and turned away.

He's going to pout until I get Tiana back. Rainek watched the princess and was struck again by her beauty. Her breasts were high and tight. The perfect complement to her tall, elegant figure. Lovely, but not Tiana. He couldn't imagine her kneeling over her lover sucking his cock while he had his tongue buried in her cunt.

Or the sweet, shocked cries that Tiana made when she'd come. As if climaxing was such a surprise. He smiled at the memory. He would give her so many climaxes that she would come to expect it, demand it of him.

"I see Tiana left you just as I'd asked. Clean and hard." She wrapped her hand around his hard cock.

And it wilted in her grasp.

Her mouth fell open as she stared at the limp rod. She cast her fierce gaze up to his. Rainek raised his eyebrows and smiled. The dragon had some uses.

Merena's jaw tightened and tiny muscles rippled along her neck as she fought to contain her irritation. "Don't worry, Your Highness," she whispered in a soft cooing tone that set Rainek's nerves on edge. "I have just the thing to make that staff hard and eager."

She released him and stepped away from the table. Then with the confidence of a woman used to the admiring glances of men, she loosened the front of her gown and pulled the sides back. The faint curves of her breasts were visible. They were lovely. With a quick shrug, she slid the material farther down until her breasts were bared. Her eyes flickered down toward his cock as if to watch his response.

Rainek did his best not to smile. She was attempting his seduction and all he could think about was Tiana and her full breasts and the tight peaks that poked against his stomach as she lain on him, her mouth wrapped around his cock. The memory inspired Denith and Rainek felt his cock twitch in response.

Merena chuckled softly. The sound was followed by the slither of silk as she let her gown fall to the ground.

His cock relaxed again. He wanted Tiana.

Get mine.

He didn't need Denith's urging. Rainek took a deep breath and found himself comparing the two women. Physically they were opposites—Tiana was short and curvy, while Merena was tall and slender.

Merena reached out again and stroked his cock. Her cool fingers were long, slim and soft. Tiana's hands were hot with rough patches, no doubt from hard labor. He wanted Tiana's hands on him.

Denith, for his part, ignored Merena. He plotted their escape and how to grab Tiana. Rainek could easily imagine the dragon pacing impatiently in his skull. But it was distracting. Denith kept putting images in his head, of Tiana writhing beneath his touch. Him pounding into her pussy. The sweet feel of her mouth on his cock. He wanted to plunge into her mouth, push his hips and force her to take more, feel her accept his come. Feel her snug cunt around his cock.

He barely noticed Merena standing beside the table until she lifted his head. "Here, Your Highness, drink this. It will make you feel better."

She poured the liquid into his mouth and he gulped to stop from choking. The sickly sweet fluid flowed down his throat but it was the smug smile on the princess's face that made his insides tighten. She wouldn't be that confident if she didn't have some plan.

"Well, now, this shouldn't take long."

A foreign pulse began to throb in his loins and he felt his cock began to fill. What in the Hells was happening?

Merena smiled and stroked her cool fingers down his growing shaft.

Denith grumbled and willed the rigidity away.

The dragon would accept no substitute.

Merena's eyes grew wide for a moment, then she leaned forward. Holding his rod in her hand, she trailed her tongue up its length. The sneering look in her eyes was enough to crush any pleasure Rainek might have found. She wasn't doing this to please him or herself but merely to make him hard enough to fuck. She opened her mouth and shoved the thick head inside. The slow swirl of her tongue was neither interesting nor exciting. Sighing, Rainek held himself still until she grew bored with her attempts. It didn't take long.

But fury lit her eyes when she pulled back. "I will have you," she announced as she straightened. She swirled her hands over his body, centered over his cock. Power penetrated his body, luring his cock to harden. The fierce arousal from whatever potion she'd fed him compounded the effect and he stared in horror as his cock began to rise. Denith battled, crushing the sensation.

Merena whispered more words and held her hands above his groin. Gammon, he thought, her witch's powers were strong.

The princess's spell flowed into his cock making it grow and lengthen. Again, Denith resisted the pull. Rainek felt like he was torn between two powers. The dragon inside him fought the magic Merena gathered, resisting with every bit of strength it possessed. The lure from Merena increased and Rainek felt a shout dragged from his chest. Glaring at her, he joined Denith in his fight, but the potion and her magic were powerful opponents.

Laughing her triumph, she climbed up on the table. "Well, my prince, it seems you desire me after all. Let us enjoy this first union."

He grit his teeth, fighting the damning pull of her spells and the aphrodisiac he'd ingested.

"Never, Princess."

She raised her eyes and the hatred in her gaze shocked him. If she hated him this much, why did she want to fuck him? It didn't make sense.

"Merena?"

The soft, familiar voice pierced Rainek's chest like an arrow.

Mine? Denith asked searching for Tiana's presence. Rainek looked toward the door. She stood in the dark opening, her hair brushed and contained, her gown tidy and clean. The dragon began to pant and Rainek felt his cock harden—for real this time.

Tiana didn't look at him. She stared at the princess.

"What?" Merena snapped.

"I'm sorry to interrupt but we have a visitor."

Merena, crouched over Rainek's cock, whipped her head around. "Who?" she snarled.

"An *important* visitor."

With an irritated sigh that bordered on being a growl, Merena crawled to the end of the table and jumped down. She didn't even glance back at him as she gathered her dress and pulled it over her head.

Tiana meanwhile, stood at the door, her eyes landing on his cock and never leaving. Her tongue flicked out, brushing the inside edge of her lip.

Rainek thought he could come right there.

"Let's go," Merena announced, grabbing Tiana by the arm and dragging her toward the hall.

The chamber door slammed shut. Denith screamed, demanding Tiana's presence.

With Merena gone, the dragon lowered his guard. Rainek's cock rose, bouncing against his stomach. He dropped his head back against the table and moaned. He needed release. He needed Tiana.

Denith latched onto that statement and began to tear at the chains, commanding Rainek's muscles to pull.

"Tiana warned us that the chains can't be broken," Rainek growled.

Wall can.

Rainek lifted his head and stared at the stone walls.

The dragon had a point.

Chapter Four

Tiana led Merena into the hall, her heart pumping from the scene she'd just witnessed — Rainek's cock hard and full, and Merena kneeling above it, ready to take him into her body. Tiana's own sex clenched. She didn't want any other to have him.

It was a silly thought brought about by the seductive whispers of a man who vowed "no one else". Not that she'd believed him, of course. What man could resist Merena's beauty?

She waited until the door was closed then turned and faced Merena.

It was selfish she knew but she was actually pleased she'd been able to interfere with a little of Merena's pleasure.

"I'm sorry to interrupt you," she felt compelled to say, even though it wasn't precisely true.

"There was nothing to interrupt. We hadn't started yet."

Strange how that assurance eased Tiana's tension.

"What do you want?"

"Her Majesty is arriving."

"What?" Merena stepped back and began to pace a tiny path along the hall. "What is she doing here? She's supposed to be in the city preparing for the prince's arrival."

Tiana shrugged. She had no idea why Queen Leika would visit the Keep. It was an isolated outpost, rarely used except by traveling members of the Matriarchy — or when a princess wanted to hide her kidnap victim, she thought grimly. Why was her home always invaded whenever someone wanted to do something they didn't want the queen to know about? But now the queen was here.

The fire in Tiana's hands fluttered. *Perfect. As if I don't have enough to deal with, I have to serve the queen.* Queen Leika mostly ignored Tiana's existence, letting her live in peace at the Keep.

"Go greet her," Merena commanded. "Say nothing of my guest. I want to surprise Her Majesty when the moment is right." She glanced toward the training chamber door. "I'll see to *him* later. By then he'll be extremely eager to have me mount him." The vengeance in Merena's voice sent shivers down Tiana's spine.

"Merena, what have you done?"

"Worried about the poor little prince?" Merena mocked. "Don't. He'll enjoy everything I do him."

"Merena, it's illegal to compel a captive—"

Merena waved Tiana's objection away. "I'm a member of the Ruling Family. I *make* the laws. It's up to others to follow them. Do not worry about the prince. I will take care of him. You should prepare for your queen."

Tiana nodded and watched as Merena spun around and walked away.

As she disappeared around a corner, Tiana fell back against the wall. She'd barely had time to go to her rooms, bathe and wash her hair before the maids had come with the report that the queen was approaching.

So, now she had a prince hidden in the training chamber, the queen on her doorstep—and after twenty-seven years of believing herself a witch with no powers, she'd discovered she was a fire witch.

Tiana opened her palms and watched the heat rise from her skin in barely visible waves.

Power comes from passion.

Merena's taunt from last night came back to Tiana as she stared blankly at the floor. A witch's powers were usually revealed during her teen years or at the latest in her early twenties. Tiana had passed those years and more with no flicker of power. It was an open secret that those closest to her ignored, choosing silence over pity.

But this was even worse. Having no power was rare and people scorned you, but being a fire witch was dangerous. Most fire witches were executed or banished. The power was too great, too dangerous.

Tiana quickly imagined smoothing her hands over Rainek's hard cock—and the resounding screams as he burnt beneath her touch.

How had this happened?

Power comes from passion.

And she'd experienced her first true passion last night. Oh, she'd been fucked before, but never had the feelings exploded within her body. Each orgasm had made the fire gather, the need greater. Now the fire coursed through her veins and there was no one to aid her.

The women of the Matriarchy feared this power so much that anyone caught using firepower against another was immediately banished or put to death.

Tiana's only consolation was that the power was easy to hide—as long as she didn't touch anyone and as long as she stayed celibate.

That wouldn't be hard. She'd managed for most of her twenty-seven years. As soon as Rainek left with Merena, the temptation he presented would be gone.

That was it, she decided. She just had to stay away from Rainek. He'd inspired this problem in the first place. If she avoided him, the power that currently surged through her body should fade.

Proud of her decision, Tiana slapped her hands against wall behind her. Steam rose from beneath her palms and a soft sizzling sound echoed across the stones. She let her hand burn against the stone, feeling the power seep from her body.

"Tiana!" Rainek's cry echoed down the hall and pushed her away from the wall. He was calling for her. She shook her head. Merena had drugged him. He was calling for any woman to fuck him.

Curling her hands into determined fists, Tiana turned away. She wouldn't be drawn back into his sensual web. It was too dangerous. For everyone involved.

* * * * *

Tiana inched farther toward the door. The Revel was in full swing and would last for hours yet. Her presence certainly wasn't needed. She'd done her duty. She'd organized the party, made sure there was food and drink for all who attended, and she'd made her curtsy to the queen. No one would notice if she slipped away. Her heart pounded inside her head. She needed a few moments alone.

The queen's arrival had prompted the Revel, bringing every woman above the most common to the Great Hall for the celebration. Merena had called for the party, saying Queen Leika's mere presence was reason enough. She'd even offered her own pleasure slaves—and those from Rainek's guard—to service those present.

If Queen Leika had been surprised to find Merena at the Keep, she'd hidden it well. Instead, she'd agreed to the party and spent the afternoon with her ladies, while Tiana had organized the blasted event.

But now, it was almost over. For her, at least. The rest of the revelers would continue through the night, choosing men to mount, swapping tales of previous lovers. Drinking all the wine in the Keep, Tiana thought with some rancor. She worked hard to keep the wine cellars well stocked to reward the guard stationed at this far outpost. Now, her reserves would be drained and the residents would drink swill until she could accumulate more.

Tiana took another step toward the door—her escape so close—and bumped into the bare chest of Harkan, one of the favored pleasure slaves.

"Sorry, Harkan," she apologized. The slave flashed her a practiced sensual smile.

"Mistress, it was my pleasure to touch you in any fashion."

It was all Tiana could do not to roll her eyes as he walked away. Harkan was very well-trained and enjoyed his work here in the Keep. The other women loved the constant sexual overtones in a well-trained slave but Tiana found it exhausting.

She knew he would have said the same thing to her no matter who she was. She looked down at her rustic green gown and the white cotton blouse she wore beneath it. It didn't match the vibrant silks and satins of the other women's gowns but Tiana knew she might be called to mop up a spill at any moment. This wasn't exactly the life she'd been born to but she enjoyed the quiet existence. If the price of that existence was occasionally playing hostess to revelers from the Queen's Court, she could accept that.

She watched as Harkan openly flirted with three women sitting on cushions. The hungry stares from the women told Tiana they were considering him for later. It might be interesting to have a true conversation with a man. One that didn't involve sex. Her thoughts instantly snapped back to Rainek. He'd talked about his family and the way he'd tortured his older brother. She smiled, remembering his stories. He hadn't yet learned that women weren't interested in a man's thoughts—only his body.

As soon as her mind wandered toward the handsome prince, she jerked it back. She was avoiding him—physically and mentally. Her hands ached with new heat. In truth, it would be better if she avoided everyone for a while. She sidled closer to the exit, casually shifting her feet until she was inches from the door.

"Where are you going?" Merena asked from over her left shoulder.

"The party is going well." Tiana offered a bright, hopefully innocent smile. "I thought I would return to my rooms. I had a late n—an early morning and with her majesty leaving tomorrow to return to the city, I should get a good night's rest."

"I need you to go check on Prince Rainek."

"What?" Tiana couldn't keep the panic out of her voice.

"I've been wrapped up with the queen all day. Someone should check on him." She smirked. "He's probably rather uncomfortable by now."

Damn it. Tiana kept the curse to herself.

"I can't leave for another few hours or so. As hostess, I'm expected to stay."

Tiana didn't point out that *she'd* done all the planning, gathering and serving but Merena was still considered the hostess. She didn't mention it, but she thought about it. Then her mind slipped back to Rainek, spread out on that table. Cock hard and eager.

"I can't believe you haven't returned to him. He's not your average captive," Tiana warned. "Sooner or later his family is going to come looking for him. I don't think they'll be pleased when he reports he was starved and *drugged*."

Merena's arrogant, slightly vicious smile made the hair along Tiana's arms stand up. "With a few of my special herbs and a spell or two, he won't remember anything I've done to him. He won't remember his own name."

Tiana shivered. Merena's power was to influence minds. That's how she'd been able to send Rainek's men to sleep so he could be captured. Tiana had no doubt that Merena could do all she claimed. But that still left Rainek in pain. Writhing in his chains, his cock hard, waiting to be fucked. Warmth pooled between her legs.

Merena glanced around the room, nodding as revelers caught her eye. The men were all naked except for the occasional loincloth. Soon, those too, would be stripped away and women would begin mounting their favorites. The queen would choose first, then Merena, as hostess, would be expected to pick hers.

"I really must stay here. Go check on him." She smirked as she folded her arms under her breasts. "I'm sure he's quite eager to see me." She licked her lips. "I think I'll forgo the offerings of the Revel and have him instead."

Tiana felt an invisible fist in her stomach at the reminder that Rainek would belong to the princess.

"Go see that he's fed and prepared. Tell him his pleasure will begin soon."

Tiana wanted to object but she couldn't. The least she could do was feed him, let him relieve himself and then assure him that Merena would come soon to ease the sexual pressure.

She nodded and turned away. She slipped from the room and hurried down the hall, an imperative emotion driving her toward him. It didn't matter that logic and self-preservation dictated that she should stay away from him—something inside her craved the sight of him. Her spirit needed to see him. She stopped in front of the door, anticipating that first glimpse of his naked body, stretched out on the table. Her core melted a little more and the warmth in her palms flared. This won't do, she mentally reprimanded herself. *You're not here for pleasure. You're here to feed and comfort.* Pushing her shoulders back, she pulled the door open and yelped.

He was gone. Truly gone.

Merena is going to be furious.

Beyond that, anyone had to be impressed. Tiana stared at the destruction of the room. The bolts that had connected the chains to the stone walls were ripped out. Chunks of rock lay scattered across the floor. The twin chains that had held Rainek were piled on the training table.

She smoothed her hand over her hair and gnawed on her lower lip. How was she going to explain this to Merena? No one had ever escaped from the training chamber before. Had the *reconi* juice somehow enraged him so much he'd had the strength to literally tear down the walls?

"Mine."

She heard the deep voice seconds before heavy hands clamped down on her shoulders and spun her around. She landed against the wall and stared up into his amber eyes. Surprise and confusion assailed her. He'd stayed. He had the chance to escape but he'd remained in the room.

"Rainek—" She never had a chance to find out what she was going to say. He was there, his mouth on hers, his tongue deep in her mouth. The invasion knocked her senses back, stunning her. The light, gentle kisses they'd exchanged last night were nothing compared to this assault on her mouth. Her will to reject him grew weak and faded even more as he curled his tongue around hers.

Delicious.

She ignored the strange voice in her head—so distracted by Rainek's command of her mouth. She couldn't fight the desire to feel all of him. She flicked her tongue against his, accepting and returning his dominating kiss.

More. Let me have more.

The plea reverberated in the pit of her stomach and it jolted her from the overwhelming pleasure of Rainek's kiss. Merena would be arriving soon to take him. His hot mouth left Tiana's and traveled along her jaw, skirting down her throat.

"Rainek, you have to stop." The sighed protest sounded false even inside her own head. But how was she supposed to resist the delicious glide of his lips across her skin? He nipped and licked and tasted as he moved until he discovered her frantically beating pulse. Then he stopped and lingered, swirling his wicked tongue across the tiny throbbing point. A shiver skittered from that place across her skin to her nipples, tightening the peaks.

Taste you. Let me taste you.

She tilted her head giving him better access even as she tried to find the strength to stop him. There were so many reasons to push him way but none were as convincing as his kisses. He moved from her neck down across her collarbone, peeling back the crisp white blouse. She had to stop him, give them both a chance to retreat. He had to understand that it was the drug making him so aroused...and she needed a moment when his lips weren't on her skin to regain her sanity.

His tongue flicked out, swiping a long stroke across her breast, close but not touching her straining nipple. When had her nipples become so sensitive?

And when had his hands slipped under her skirts?

She gasped as one huge palm cupped her bare backside, pulling her close, bringing her into contact with the thick line of his cock. She instinctively opened her legs, preparing a place for him. He slipped into the vee she'd created and thrust gently — his hard cock teasing her sex. Tiana dragged in a breath. She had to get control. Truly she did. And she would...as soon as he stopped rubbing that wicked shaft between her thighs.

She tried again. "Please, Prince Rainek, you don't understand..."

"Want you," he growled.

"No, you don't. If you'll let me—" His hand plunged between her legs, driving his finger into her wet sex. "Uh, no, Rainek you don't understand...you're supposed to, oh by the Goddesses." He stroked the inside of her sex, teasing it. Loving it. "No, really, you mustn't." He repeated the same tickling action. "Oh my." Another wave hit her, sending her head against the wall behind her. Grateful for its support, she placed one hand on the wall and one on his shoulder — the two solid objects in her world. "Please, Rainek." She had to make him see reason. Before she did something stupid. Like let him come inside her.

It would be bad on so many levels.

His thumb moved forward, stroking her tight clit.

And good on so many others.

"Rainek, you have to stop. Merena gave you a…a drug. That's what's making you want to…"

Mine. She knew something was wrong. The voices in her head were growing louder but even that didn't stop the pulsing need between her legs. He added a second finger inside her pussy and began to pump, slowly in and out. She tried to ignore the seductive pressure and focus on what she needed to say.

"Rainek, please, the potion Merena gave you was a drug…an aphrodisiac. That's what's making you want to…fuck."

"You. Want you."

"No, it's the drug."

You.

The voice was insistent. And in that moment she realized, she wasn't hallucinating. He'd spoken with her…without actually speaking. She shook her head and stared at Rainek. As if he noticed her observation, he raised his head and looked into her eyes. She flinched at the change. Gone was the fire-warmed amber gaze she'd admired before. In its place was black—soulless darkness. Before she could scream, it was gone and color returned. Rainek seemed to return with it.

"Let me have you. I have to have you." His words were soft and gentle and they tore down the last of her resistance with the fury of a hurricane. She couldn't stand against it. "Let me have you," he said again.

Though she knew it was the drug talking—that he would be this desperate for any woman who had entered the chamber—she couldn't find the will to resist.

Rainek knew the moment she accepted him. Her fear left her and her passion overtook her worries. He bent down and once again captured her mouth in a long, tongue-binding kiss.

More. Let me have more.

Rainek forced the dragon from his head. *Mine,* he snarled, directing the thought to Denith. Tiana would belong to him first. The beast pushed but didn't overwhelm him. He knew Denith could, if he chose, command the body they shared. But the dragon held back, demanding only that Rainek move ahead.

I want my turn with her — want my tongue in her.

Rainek nodded, giving Denith the silent promise of access to the delicious cunt that called to them both.

Rainek pushed her skirts farther out of the way. The delightful scent of her sex called to him — she'd been so warm and responsive when he'd tasted her — but he needed to feel her wrapped around his cock, needed to feel the sweet clinging walls of her pussy holding him.

He continued to stroke her with his fingers. She was wet and slick.

"Let me have you," he whispered against her neck. "I need to come inside you."

She groaned and tilted her head to the side, allowing him access to the sensitive curve of her throat. "Yes." Her agreement was so soft he almost missed it but his body heard. He reached down and grabbed the long heavy skirts that covered her. He needed to see her sweet limbs, feel her ass pressed against him as he pumped into her. He jerked the gown up and over her head, tossing it casually behind him. The white cotton blouse remained behind, barely reaching the tops of her thighs. The outline of her tight nipples was clear against the material. She blinked up at him in surprise.

Rainek smiled. She seemed stunned yet she hadn't run from him. He arched his hips forward, sliding his shaft between her legs, not entering her but feeling the sweet liquid of her cunt drip down, coating her thighs and lubricating his cock.

Her green eyes blinked as he pumped his shaft into the deep crevice between her thighs. She wanted this. Her soul screamed for this as his did. He could see it in her eyes, in the hungry way she watched him. Soon, he promised silently, directing the vow to her and to his dragon.

He pulled the front placket of her blouse open—tearing at the laces that held her bodice closed—and revealed her full, heavy breasts. He hadn't tasted them before—only her delicious cunt—but now he would. A small sample now. Later he would spend hours worshiping her breasts. He bent down and slurped one tight peak into his mouth. The startled catch of her breath made him repeat the motion and this time she moaned.

Delicious, Denith encouraged.

Yes. The temptation to linger on her nipples tugged at him but he knew he had to resist. The other witch could arrive anytime but he couldn't leave before he'd come inside Tiana. He'd waited too long...and Denith would wait no longer.

Rainek pulled back, dragging his cock away from the warmth of her pussy. The soft brush of her hair teased him and made him long to drive into her but he needed her another way. He needed to ride her hard. Thirty years of frustration had built an intense need in his body. He would be a gentle, gentlemanly lover later.

Now, he needed to fuck her.

"Mine," he announced, hooking his hand on her hip and spinning her around. Her palms slapped against the wall, catching her weight as he turned her. A faint sizzling sound as if someone had thrown meat onto a fire filled the chamber but the sweet curve of her ass against his stomach drew his thoughts away from the noise.

Tiana released a soft moaning sigh and pressed her hips back as if offering her cunt to him. A red mist floated over his mind. A vague memory of his father's description of making love to his mate under the dragon's influence surfaced. Rainek pushed it away to consider later. He needed to fuck his woman.

He placed the head of his cock against her opening. The tenuous control he'd maintained so far snapped as he felt her hot, wet passage ease for him. He drove forward, thrusting deep, penetrating her cunt. His howl bounced off the chamber walls as she welcomed his entrance, clinging to him. He held himself still, savoring the tight hold, listening to her breath coming in harsh pants from her lips. He nudged his hips forward, settling his shaft a fraction deeper. A tiny catch in the back of her throat made him hesitate.

"Hurt you?" he asked, finding himself only able to speak in Denith's single syllable grunts.

She shook her head. "Feels good," she answered in the same gasping way. "Big." They stood, each waiting for a sign from the other to continue.

Rainek bent his head and began to place light kisses along her neck, her shoulders—trying to draw on human strength, resisting the dragon's urge to fuck her until she couldn't walk. He waited, then felt it—a slight roll of her hips as if she wanted more, wanted him deeper. The delicate movement flooded his senses.

He didn't have the strength or the patience for a slow delicate fuck. He held her hips, his fingers digging into her curved flesh, and pulled back. With a long, hard thrust he slammed into her. And was rewarded with a groaned approval.

"Yes," she whimpered, pressing against the wall and moving in sweet opposition. Each stroke sent him deeper. And she took him, took all that he gave. The depths of his soul erupted in triumph. This was the woman made for him. The woman who craved his cock as much as he did her pussy.

Years of abstinence pushed him to coming but he wanted her to enjoy the moment as well. He reached around and placed his hand against her mound, quickly finding the swollen flesh of her clit. He cupped her pussy and held her, giving her something to rub against as they moved together. The soft hitches in her breath were growing louder—every thrust taking him deep inside. This was what he was made for—being inside this woman. Becoming one with her.

Tiana couldn't get enough air into her lungs or enough distance in her mind. Whatever he was doing to her had captured all her senses, commanding her will, her desire. It had been more than a year since she'd allowed anyone to enter her and now the full penetration of his cock was so much more than she'd ever experienced. She arched her back, needing him deeper, wanting more of him.

His hand pressed against her clit. She pumped downward, loving the delicious friction of his fingers along her sex—his cock filling her, his fingers stroking the soft flesh.

"Harder," she whispered. "More."

He pushed deeper, faster. Harder. Tiana braced herself and let him pound into her. It was what she wanted. Release was close. She could feel it and reached for it. The pressure swirled around her clit, called forth by his touch and the frantic thrust into her pussy. She couldn't hold it back. Wicked pleasure shattered within her, like a waterfall scattering bright shiny drops through her cunt and into her limbs. She gasped and sagged against the wall, her cheek brushing the cool surface.

"Oh, baby, you feel so good around my cock. Come for me again. Come for me."

His touch on her clit was light as if he knew how sensitive she was even as he pumped deeper inside her. On the dying edges of her climax, another one struck. She straightened her knees and forced her hips back, driving him deeper inside her.

"Let me come inside you."

"Yes," she said, her voice harsh and low.

With a long heavy groan, he released his seed. It flowed into her in hot waves, pulsing into her sex. Rainek's hands covered hers, his fingers entwining with hers as they pressed against the wall. He leaned around and placed hot kisses along her neck. His cock was still hard inside her.

"Mine," he whispered against her ear.

Shivers ran down her spine. There was something dangerous about that word. His hand brushed across her shoulder.

"Forgive me," he said.

Blackness covered her mind.

* * * * *

Rainek released his pinch on her shoulder as Tiana sank to the ground. He hated to do that to her but he had to get her out of here, and while she'd seemed quite willing to fuck him, he didn't think she'd be as willing to help him escape. He'd kept his word. He'd promised her last night that he wouldn't attempt to escape *that night*. It was a new moon rise and that gave him leave to free himself.

Denith had been right about the walls. They'd collapsed under the dragon's awesome strength. And even the bands around his wrists had snapped with enough pressure. The princess had obviously only hexed the chains. She hadn't thought about the other parts of the equation.

During the hours after he'd freed himself, he'd searched the room and gathered a few items he would need. A blanket, a knife, a cup for water. He dropped them into a woven sack along with a worn pair of leathers he'd found stuffed in a cupboard. His own clothes were gone but thankfully his amulet had been left behind. He considered contacting his brother but didn't want the distraction. Bren would insist on hearing about Tiana and Rainek wanted to enjoy her for a little longer before he shared her with his family.

Slinging the bag over his shoulder, he bent down, lifted Tiana into his arms and stepped into the hall. Allowing Denith's senses to work, he listened to the rowdy voices at the far end of the corridor. A party. Even better. No one would come looking for him.

Rainek carried his mate down the hall and took the first passage that smelled like fresh air. The moment he cleared the building, he placed Tiana on the ground and put the bag beside her. With a sigh, he let his head fall back.

He hated this.

The dragon's power rose inside him. Denith exploded, filling the twilight with his cry and taking on his corporeal form. Rainek felt a moment's disorientation then returned to find himself locked in the dragon's body.

Denith swung his head toward Tiana and his tongue flickered out. *Mine.*

Yes, but get us out of here, Rainek urged. *Then you can have her.*

The dragon was irritated but not illogical. He gently collected his tiny mate in his claws, held her against his chest and leapt into the air.

Chapter Five

Tiana woke slowly, drifting to wakefulness with the vague knowledge that she wasn't in her chambers on her slightly lumpy bed. She was on a hard surface. Rock-hard. And her body ached, her head throbbed and her shoulders were tight. Even without opening her eyes, she knew she was bound. Tied with her hands stretched above her. A faint breeze slipped across her skin warning her she was naked. Her nipples tightened beneath the cool air. Definitely naked.

The situation seemed eerily familiar and her heart began to thud loudly in her chest

The last thing she remembered was walking in to the training chamber.

Rainek. Tiana allowed her eyes to ease open. Darkness surrounded her giving her no hint of where she was. Was she even still at the Keep? She tried to remember what had happened.

She'd been staring at the destruction of the walls when he'd grabbed her, kissed her, fucked her—making her come—twice—and then her memory went blank. He'd obviously brought her here, stripped her naked.

An unwanted excitement fluttered through her sex. Rainek. He'd taken her hard—and with a wild intensity. Like a boy with a new toy. Of course this boy had a nine-inch cock that was thick and hard. And it had been inside her. Deep inside her. She began to heat between her legs with the memory. Unable to contain it, she moaned softly.

Are you in pain? Or is it your desire that makes you groan?

She gasped and lifted her head, trying to see into the darkness, searching for whoever had spoken. There was no one there. At least no one she could see.

A weak torch jammed into a crack in the wall illuminated the small area near her. Straining her neck up, she scanned the space she could see. Rock floor, rock walls, rock ceiling. She was in some sort of roughly hewn cavern. Though she couldn't see it all, it appeared massive. She pulled on the ropes and found they gave easily, allowing her to place her hands on the ground rock beside her. She pushed herself up to sitting and looked around. Dim light from the cave entrance teased her eyes but something seemed to cover the opening. Nothing moved. No one spoke. She was alone.

Except for the voice in her head.

She moved her hands forward but there wasn't enough play in the ropes to allow her hands to meet. She lay back down. A blanket had been put beneath her giving her some protection from the stone floor. As she raised her hands in front of her face and concentrated on the knots around her wrists, she realized that the burning sensation was gone. She had a faint memory of fire while Rainek was inside her but sleep seemed to have eased the pain.

Like so many other things, she pushed the thought into the back of her mind, promising herself that she would consider it later after she'd gotten free. And murdered Prince Rainek. How dare he kidnap her and tie her up? Naked. Her conscience immediately pointed out the similarities between her situation and his. Admittedly, Merena had done much the same thing to him but that didn't justify Tiana getting drawn into it. She'd helped but only under duress.

Rainek doesn't know that, her overly developed conscience pointed out. Damn, it did no good to blame him. He merely wanted his revenge. But, by the Hells, this wasn't her plan. She had been on the edges of this plot.

Right up to the point you allowed him to fuck you. She winced. That was going to get her into trouble. Seducing a consort was one of the highest crimes in the land. It didn't matter that she hadn't seduced him — that he'd been the seducer — the result would be the same. Unless she could get herself out of here. Then the worst thing they could lay at her feet was letting him escape. And after the damage done to the walls, she didn't think anyone would blame her. By the Goddesses, how had he managed to do that? He'd pulled the stones from the wall.

Her fingers plucked at the ropes but the knots held firm. She pulled her lips back and growled in frustration.

Are you hurt?

She stopped. The voice filled her head, without echoing through the room. What was going on? She struggled to see into the shadows but all was darkness. The whisper of scales across stone piqued her interest. *Scales? What in all the Hells is out there?*

"Who are you?" she demanded. "Step out so I can see you."

The swish grew louder. Tiana watched as the biggest creature she'd ever imagined walked forward, blocking the weak sunlight from the cave entrance.

The beast's purple and blue head was as large as her whole body — with white, sharp — very sharp — teeth. She didn't need to see beyond the glowing eyes to know she'd been captured by a dragon.

Oh Goddesses. When had that happened? Where was Rainek? Had he been injured? Killed? She wanted to look around the dark, to search for Rainek's broken body, but she didn't dare take her eyes off the huge beast that stood before her.

The dragon continued its slow, lumbering pace forward, until it stood just beyond her feet. Its large head swung toward her, hovering over her prone body. The long dark pink tongue flicked out and ran around the beast's mouth.

Tiana felt her heart leap into her throat. She'd heard the stories. She'd always wondered if they were true. Now, with one of the creatures standing over her, she realized she could become a dragon's victim. The bloody, battered bodies of women who'd been sacrificed to dragons were legend. No one knew precisely what the dragons did to the women, only that many preferred death. If they survived, they were often insane, changed forever, broken and begging to return to the dragon. But by then the dragon had moved on.

Tiana pulled on the ropes, clawing at the knots at her wrists. If she could just get free she might have a chance. The Grand Forest that surrounded the Keep—and she had to believe that Prince Rainek hadn't carried her too far beyond the Matriarchy lands—would give her cover to escape. Somehow she didn't think the dragon would be able to move quickly amid the trees.

Do not harm yourself. I told Rainek it was not necessary to tie you down but he didn't believe me.

Rainek? He knew about the dragon? Had he kidnapped her with the intention of sacrificing her to a dragon? Tiana ignored the low melodious voice in her head assuring her that she was safe and continued to pull. Her panic gave her strength. Too many tales rampaged through her head. She would be killed or broken by this beast.

Of course, didn't dragon sacrifices have to be virgins? She didn't qualify. She hadn't qualified *before* last night but she definitely didn't after having Rainek inside her. She'd been well and truly fucked. Another jolt of remembered pleasure infiltrated her sex.

She had to get out of here. She spun her hand around and grabbed the rope that connected her to the wall. Maybe she could fray it.

Hmmm. I can smell your desire. Delicious.

The voice changed, becoming deeper with a hunger that resounded through her body. It was almost the same sensation as when Rainek had begged for her cunt.

She had to get out of here, away from the ravening beast that was going to rip her limb from limb. Tiana continued her frantic struggle for freedom, but kept her eyes on the creature.

The dragon tilted his head and calmly watched her struggles as if amused by her attempts. With a fatalistic sigh, she finally collapsed down. There was no way to free herself and even if she did, the dragon would block her escape.

"Fine, kill me." Feeling noble and brave, she turned her head to the side and waited for the death blow.

It almost sounded like a chuckle in her head and by the Hells, the noise sounded familiar. *Why would I want to do that?*

The question was followed by a deliberate swipe of the dragon's tongue across her thigh, and the tip of her sex. Her gasp echoed across the silent cave. She opened her eyes. The dragon's head hovered above her. As she watched, the long pink tongue flicked out and swirled around her nipple, bringing it to a tight point.

Despite her best intentions, her pussy began to weep. The memory of Rainek's mouth and his cock—plunging into her, riding her deeply—reminded her of what real pleasure could be. She willed herself to block out the delicious memories and continued to pull on the ropes. It gave her something to do besides stare at the beast that was about to devour her.

The next teasing touch snapped her attention away from her hands...and right between her legs. His tongue poked out of his mouth and raked across the inside of her thigh.

Delicious.

Tiana waited, knowing what was about to happen but still shocked at the possibility. Surely he wasn't going to...? The slow licks continued up into the folds of her sex and flicking with delicate intensity across her clit. She couldn't stop the low rumble of pleasure that started in her throat.

"Please," she begged, trying to twist her legs and close them. The dragon looked up and Tiana endured another surprise. He looked hurt, as if her rejection pained him.

Why? Do you not want it? Do you not feel the pleasure?

The sadness in his words distracted her long enough for him to bend down and once again insinuate his tongue between her legs. This time the nimble length forged its way into her cunt, teasing the inside of her passage. Her breath caught in her throat and she stared up at the stone ceiling. She should be fighting, resisting, but her body wouldn't respond to the appropriate commands of her mind. His touch felt good, too good to resist. As if sensing her compliance, the dragon pushed forward, sinking farther inside her. She gasped and grabbed the ropes that held her, keeping her body taut.

Open for me.

The whispered command was accompanied by a rumble deep inside her sex. Following her body's demand for more, she widened her legs. The dragon took immediate advantage and nuzzled his snout forward, pressing against the apex of her thighs.

You enjoyed Rainek's cock. The dragon's voice rumbled with pleasure. *Now, it is my turn to have you.*

She barely understood the words but she could sense the creature's desire. He pumped his tongue inside her, mimicking the motion of a cock, plunging deep and caressing the inside walls deep in her cunt. He massaged the upper wall of her passage—reaching where no one had before. The sensation shot through her cunt. Tiana cried out—her climax hitting her like brilliant sunburst. Moisture flowed from her sex. The sound of her groan blended with the satisfied growl of the dragon. She blinked and tried to recapture her soul.

How had the creature done that? And, it appeared it wasn't done yet.

Yes. More. Give me more.

He pulled from her passage and lapped at her pussy—capturing and creating more of the hot viscous liquid that flowed from her pussy. Still awash in sensation, she couldn't protest. He licked her slit, tracing delicate patterns across her wet flesh, tripping up to circle her clit.

Her hands burned but she had no way to control it, not while the dragon continued. Time faded. She was distantly aware that the light at cave entrance was brighter but the dragon consumed her senses, licking and tasting her until she shivered with each stroke, twisted to reach more of him.

He dragged his tongue along the inside of her outer lips, the light abrasion alerting every nerve. He lingered long, tracing her pussy, teasing her and tempting her, dipping into her cunt and massaging the inside edge. He seemed to know where to touch to keep her on the verge of climax. Never allowing her that blessed relief.

"Please!" she finally begged.

He circled her clit, drawing it out, then covered the tight bundle with his tongue, stoking it in tiny, delicate pulses. It was almost like he was sucking on it but the sensation went deeper.

Tiana felt her eyes widen. She stared into the dark and tried to keep her body from shattering but the dragon's unrelenting pull on her clit crushed her resistance. She panted, trying to gather enough air. Her hips pumped in time with his suckling. Bending her knees, she unconsciously opened herself. The beast grumbled in pleasure and seemed to reward her, driving his tongue into her pussy.

The deep penetration threw her once again into the bright explosion of climax. She heard a groan and knew somewhere in the depths of her mind that the sound had come from her.

She returned to herself to find the dragon licking the inside her of thighs, as if amusing himself until she was calm again. She stared up in amazement. The black eyes glowed yellow for a moment—a strangely familiar amber.

Before she could assimilate the information, he started again—pushing inside her passage. He didn't fill her the way Rainek had but the pressure was incredible, deep inside her pussy, he swirled the tip, teasing the far inside walls of her cunt. As if the entire center of her being was being caressed. Tiana bolted upright, her knees clamping around the dragon's head. She stared down at the creature, amazed that he could create such power, inspire so many sensations in her body. He didn't stop. He rumbled his pleasure and the sound vibrated into her pussy.

She tightened her fingers around the ropes that held her and felt the flames begin. Within seconds the twisted strands were gone, burned by her fire. Freed, she let her hands fall to the stone floor beneath her, holding herself upright as she endured more and more. He wasn't letting the pleasure stop. With each flick of his tongue, he pushed her higher.

Mine. Give me more. Fluid gushed from the center of her body as she reached another peak. The scream that was lodged in the back of her throat came out as a whimper as her body reached its limit and she collapsed onto the blanket, her legs spread wide, open to whatever the dragon wanted. Her body, her mind, her spirit were empty. An exhaustion that went far beyond the physical tugged at her.

The warm wet stroke of his tongue lapping the inside of her thigh made her whimper. She couldn't take much more, but neither could she refuse him. He made no move to enter her, or even tease her clit. His caresses were soft, almost comforting. She let her hands drop to the stone floor, her eyelids falling shut.

Yes, sleep now, my one. More later.

Though it wasn't a question, she groaned her agreement. There would be more later. The soft touch lulled her into sleep where dreams chased her. Dreams of dragons and fire.

* * * * *

Rainek sat on a rock and glared morosely at the sleeping woman before him. He wasn't mad at her. It wasn't her fault that Denith had fucked her to exhaustion. But there was no way to glare at the dragon in his head.

Rainek shifted, his cock hard and straining against the too-small leathers he'd stolen from the keep. He hadn't had time to check for fit and damn, there wasn't enough room for his cock. Especially not when it was hard. Which it was and had been since Denith had retreated and Rainek had returned to human form. Though he hadn't been in charge when Denith had tongue-fucked Tiana, he'd been present and could feel the dragon's arousal and satisfaction at having brought her to climax so many times. Even the flavor of her sex lingered on his mouth.

He wanted to taste her for himself, without the veil of the dragon between them. But he couldn't. Not until she was rested.

Denith growled contentedly in his head. Rainek could almost picture the dragon snuggled into a corner of his mind, sighing and smiling. A dragon's arousal and need were satisfied by the fluids of a woman's cunt. And Denith had certainly received enough from Tiana to keep him sated for a while.

Want more.

Rainek rolled his eyes. "You'll have to wait." He waved his hand toward the blankets. "Look what you've done. Neither of us can have her." She'd managed somehow to tear through the ropes he'd used to bind her and was curled on her side, her head resting on her arm. Her legs were drawn up revealing the full curve of her ass and a hint of the delightfully pink, wet sex that Denith had sampled. Rainek licked his lips and Denith's memory settled on his tongue.

Yes. More. Let's have more.

The dragon's arousal combined with Rainek's, making his cock harder and even more uncomfortable.

"She needs sleep," he said. He stroked his hand over his crotch unable to stop himself. The thick leather blocked most of the sensation. Sounds of Tiana's sighs and that wicked gasp when she came filled his mind. The noises were soon accompanied by visual images of her writhing on the floor close to orgasm. *Denith.*

Even though it hadn't actually happened to Rainek, the dragon's memories became his as the creature replayed them in his mind, repeating over and over again her moments of shocked pleasure.

He felt the blood drain from his head and it all seemed to flow toward his groin. The images kept replaying. Without thinking, he opened the leathers and pulled out his cock. Tiana moaned softly in her sleep. Was she reliving the experience in her dreams? Knowing he would just make himself more uncomfortable but unable to stop, he began to stroke his cock, staring at her, remembering the dragon's loving. She rolled over, ending on her back, her hands curling beside her head as her legs fell open. The action was followed by a discontented groan as if she didn't want to be awakened. He stared at the tuft of blonde hair covering her sex.

More. Let us have more.

Rainek felt himself rise at Denith's insistence but quickly replanted his butt on the rock. "I can't. She needs rest."

She needs us. Look. She's wet. Delicious.

Rainek held his cock in one hand, needing the firm grip as he watched his woman. Weak light made the liquid around her sex glitter. Was she wet? He extended his senses, using Denith's superior sight and smell, and was instantly awash in fresh stimuli. Her scent, the color of her flesh and the lovely feminine moisture called to him. He let the sensations fill him. Gods, he wanted her.

Focused solely on her, he rose, stripped off the leathers and dropped them on the stone floor. He moved closer, just needing to be near her. Denith remained silent but Rainek sensed the dragon's smug triumph. He didn't care. He had to have her. Had to taste the flesh between her legs and penetrate her with his cock. Fill her with his seed. The drive was too strong to ignore. Slowly, he placed his hand on her ankle. Warmth exploded into his palm.

Just a taste.

"Just a taste," Rainek repeated. He stroked his fingers up the inside of her legs, teasing the backs of her knees. She shifted at the light touch, unconsciously spreading her legs wider. Rainek stared at her cunt. He continued, sending caresses upward, silently encouraging her to open more for him.

* * * * *

Tiana drew in a deep breath and tried not to react. She was supposed to be asleep. And she had been until she'd heard Rainek speaking. She couldn't figure out who he was talking to but she assumed it was the dragon. Somehow Prince Rainek had managed to tame a dragon.

She'd hoped to hear his plan for her but instead he'd talked about letting her sleep before having her again. Despite her best intentions, her body had responded. Her pussy was wet. And aching. Amazing as it seemed, she wanted more. It did no good to tell her logical mind that she'd been kidnapped and tied her down and that she shouldn't want this. The memory of Rainek's cock inspired her to desire more.

As she lay still, he spread her sex wide with his fingers and placed his pointed tongue against her clit. With delicate assurance, he massaged one side, sending streaks of pleasure deep into her sex. She couldn't hold back the groan that crept from her chest. She felt him smile against her skin but the steady strokes continued, each caress giving her more. She didn't know how much more she could take. Her body was limp from the almost vicious tonguing that the dragon had given her and now it was starting again.

She pressed her fingers into her palms. The heat was incredible. The little nap she'd taken had done nothing to reduce the fire in her veins and now Rainek was making it worse. She'd be lucky if she didn't burn down the cave by the time he was finished.

But if the rocks burned down around his head, he only had himself to blame, she thought smugly. He was the one who'd kidnapped a fire witch after all. His touch was different from what the dragon had done but no less powerful. And she didn't want it to stop. Not yet.

Giving up all pretense of being asleep, she slowly pumped her hips up, silently demanding more. He opened his mouth over her clit and sucked, groaning as he pulled the tight bit of flesh between his lips. Tiana arched up on her shoulders as the pulses erupted from her sex.

He trailed his tongue up her slit as if gathering a final taste before moving on. Her frazzled brain screamed in protest. He couldn't stop now. She needed more. There had to be more.

Rainek placed a soft kiss on her mound and then rose above her. Her legs curled instinctively to accept his hips as he knelt between them. She stared down between their bodies. His cock stood dark and hard, ready to fuck. He placed the thick head against her entrance, rubbing the tip against the clit he'd just sucked to life.

Rainek stared down at his beautiful mate. She'd been so hot and delicious but now she watched him with wary eyes. It was as if she didn't understand what was going to happen. A moment of panic sliced through his heart. Was she preparing to push him away? The concern was instantly captured by Denith and magnified as the dragon's innate fear of rejection exploded.

"Mine," Rainek heard himself growl. "Have mine."

Tiana flinched and pulled back, if not physically then sensually. Rainek commanded Denith to withdraw and then leaned forward, holding himself over her but not entering her. Though his body screamed to fuck her, he knew he had to go slow. He didn't want a mate who feared him.

He placed a gentle kiss on her mouth. "You're so delicious. Do you want my cock inside you?"

Not giving her a chance to answer, he kissed her again, her mouth, her cheeks, gently loving her despite the driving need to fuck her. He moved down her body. Her full breasts were heavy. He'd imagined them filling his hands. Pushing up on his knees he cupped her breasts in his palms, squeezing gently, then with more power as she sighed. The tight peaks poked up. A new taste to enjoy, he thought as he leaned forward and lightly smoothed his tongue first over one nipple and then the other.

Her sweet sigh revealed that Tiana liked the soft brush of his tongue on her breasts. He opened his mouth and captured her nipple, applying the same suction he'd given her clit. She moaned and rolled her hips as if begging for his cock.

He leaned back and wrapped his hand around his shaft, directing the head toward her pussy. As he started to slip inside, she tensed beneath him. Again.

"What's wrong, honey?" He stopped his penetration. "Don't you want me?" He silently swore he was willing—and able—to pull back if she told him no, but he wasn't sure that was truth. Even in the weak light, Rainek could see a faint blush on her cheeks. She squirmed and an inch of his cock sank into her. The sensation stopped them both but then she looked up at him.

"I don't know how to do this."

He glanced down at the blankets, their bodies, his cock, her pussy. Then he returned to her face.

"We've done it before," he said, thoroughly confused. She'd done just fine when he'd had her in the training chamber. And when Denith had had her.

"Not—" She indicated to the potential connection of their bodies. "—Like this."

He shook his head.

"With you on top of me. I've never done it before."

Rainek felt his lips pull up into a wide grin. It wasn't a reaction he could control. The women of her world were used to riding their men. The idea had merit and Rainek knew he wanted to enjoy that position as well but for this time he needed to thrust. Needed to be able to move and drive deep into her.

"It's the first time I've been on top of you." He eased his hips against hers, pushing more of his cock into her. She was slippery. He hadn't lost her interest. Her pussy was so wet for him. "But you know we fit together." He kissed her mouth, her chin, along her jaw. "You hold me so tight within your beautiful little cunt." He reached between them and tickled her clit with his fingertip. "We'll figure out how to make it work together."

The confusion eased in her gaze and the glaze of passion quickly returned.

Rainek was halfway inside her. He stopped and waited. She felt so good he wanted to drive deep into her but he waited, needing her approval. Needing her permission.

He watched her eyes droop and his heart almost exploded in his chest. She was such a sensual creature. He continued, penetrating her, impaling her. When he'd had her in the chamber, he'd been so focused on fucking her—on coming inside her—now, he could enjoy her, feel every inch of her pussy.

Slowly he drew back pausing only a breath before he sank back into her. He went deeper, allowing more of his cock to sink into her. He kept up the slow steady penetration, each time taking more of her. Her slick passage eased with each thrust. She felt so good, the long lovely grip of her pussy clinging to every inch. Almost fully inside her, he pulled back and thrust back in.

Tiana arched her neck and grabbed at the blankets beneath her. The muscles in her arms and shoulders pulled tight as she tugged on the material under her hips. He recognized the passion in her eyes but wanted to feel her hands on him, feel her hold him and clutch him to her.

"Don't you like the feel of me inside you?" he whispered rocking his hips to settle deeper. The fit was so tight he couldn't stop. "Tell me, baby. Do you want me to leave you?"

He could sense Denith's distress but Rainek knew the answer. Tiana's body told him the truth, even if she hadn't said the words.

He started to pull away, needing the words, needing something more from her.

"No!" Her hands fluttered as if she was going to reach for him but she stopped. Her legs wrapped around his waist and her heels dug into his ass. "Don't leave me."

There was no way to resist her plea—or the heavy-lidded lust-filled look in her eyes.

He plunged into her pussy and lost himself in the pulse of fucking her. Nothing else mattered. Only Tiana—her cries filling his ears—cries of pleasures and cries for more.

Years of frustration exploded through his loins. This was the fucking he'd dreamed of. Her legs around him, pulling him deep inside her—as deep as he could go. Her slick cunt welcoming each thrust. He heard her cry out and felt the soft flickers of her orgasm but he didn't, couldn't stop. He needed more.

He continued to ride her, pulling climax after climax from her until she was limp and sobbing, begging for more, begging for him to stop. The sweet cries massaged his shaft like a fist and he drove in one final time. The sharp clear pleasure of his own orgasm rode down his spine like a cat's claws and burst from his cock, filling his mate with his seed. He fell on top of her, burying his face in her neck as he groaned the deep satisfaction of release.

Tiana accepted his heavy weight on top of her, her arms and legs cradling him. The frantic beat of his pulse thudded through his chest into hers, taking control of her heart and making it beat in the same rhythm. When his slowed, hers did as well.

She was almost sure he'd fallen asleep—on top of her. Inside her.

Her eyes fell shut and she considered following him into that blessed state. Sleep would be good. Her body was exhausted and her hands burning with every layer of the Hells. She would no doubt set fire to him if she touched him.

It would be one way of escaping, she thought, but immediately rejected the idea. She couldn't hurt Rainek. He hadn't hurt her. Not yet. Well, he'd let a dragon touch her but the dragon hadn't actually hurt her either. Tiana curled her fingers into tight fists, containing the flame.

Rainek's mouth brushed her neck and across her jaw. Finally he lifted his head and smiled. The dazed, almost goofy look in his eyes made her heart flip-flop. "You're amazing." He kissed her lips. "You take all of me and offer so much in return."

She felt herself blush at the strange compliment.

Rainek rolled over, sliding his body off hers and slipping his softening rod from between her legs. "You need to sleep," he whispered. "Let me hold you." To accompany his words, he dragged her over him pulling her practically on top so that he lay beneath her. His chest was almost as hard as the stone floor, but much warmer.

Moments before the thought of sleep had been a tempting vision, now, it pulled on her with inexorable strength. Warm and cosseted, she couldn't resist its lure and found herself fading into that sweet darkness.

* * * * *

Tiana awoke slowly to the sound of rustling. It wasn't the hiss of dragon scales but the sound of someone moving around. She opened her eyes and saw Rainek kneeling by a small fire. He tossed a thin stick on the dancing flame. She watched for a moment before he turned to her. His quick smile sent new shivers down her spine. He'd had her, fucked until her thighs were bruised. And he was still with her, smiling. When he saw she was awake, he stood and came to her side.

"Would you like something to eat? There are some dahla fruit trees nearby." He placed some of the smooth green fruit on a small cloth next to her. Pulling the blanket up, she covered herself to her chest and sat up. She wasn't used to such blatant nakedness. It didn't matter that Rainek had seen her naked — had touched her body in the most intimate ways.

Rainek smiled as if her modesty was a sweet thing then pulled out a dagger and began to slice the fruit, peeling back the thick skin and revealing the black flesh underneath. Juice dripped from his fingers. Tiana licked her lips imagining the sweet sticky flavor in her mouth. Her nipples hardened as she watched him. Every action a sensual feast — every movement slow and deliberate.

She accepted the fruit he peeled for her and took the sexual reprieve to think about her situation. In the semi-dark of the cave, there was no way to tell how much time had passed. The hours blurred together, made hazy by the pleasure.

She'd been kidnapped at night. But when the dragon had appeared, the morning light had been creeping through the cave entrance. She glanced in that direction. Darkness filled the space beyond the fire. That would mean it was nighttime. Or that the huge dragon was blocking the entrance.

Despite all the pleasure she'd received both from the dragon and Rainek, she had to return to the Keep. She could only hide her condition for so long before he realized her hands were practically on fire. At least at the Keep she could isolate herself. Eventually the flames would fade away. And if she stayed celibate, it was likely they wouldn't return. Obviously, she didn't even have to stay completely celibate. Her previous lovers hadn't inspired her power. Only Rainek.

The sooner she got away from him, the sooner things would return to normal.

But that meant never fucking Rainek again. Pain filled her chest and sank down, into her sex. Never to have him inside her again.

She took another bite of fruit and tried to ignore the ache. Unless she wanted to spend her life hiding from others, she had to get away from him.

Somehow she had to get past Rainek and the dragon. Only she didn't know where the dragon was at the moment. Probably waiting outside while Rainek fucked her.

"Where's the dragon?" She bit into the sweet fruit and watched him. Rainek hesitated for a moment then shrugged.

"He's near."

That answer was completely unenlightening.

"Why do you do it?" He seemed like an honorable man yet here he was.

Rainek swallowed and shook his head.

"Do what?"

"Kidnap women and sacrifice them to dragons."

She didn't expect his bark of laughter. "Sacrifice?" The arrogant smile that curved Rainek's mouth made the tiny hairs along her neck stand up. He was mocking her. "You weren't exactly an unwilling victim," he pointed out, laughter hovering just below his words.

Her eyes grew round and Rainek knew he'd made a serious tactical mistake.

"You were watching? You knew what he was doing and you didn't stop him?" She dropped the blanket she'd been hiding under, rolled over and stood up in one fluid motion. For a moment he thought she'd run, but she didn't. She glared down at him. She seemed to have forgotten she was naked. Rainek had not. Particularly when her pussy was inches above his mouth and Denith was planting specific suggestions about what he could do. "How could you stand by and watch that...that creature do that to me?"

The irritation in her words drew his attention higher up, to her eyes — blazing with anger.

He leaned back, putting his palms against the floor behind him. It was a great position to stare at her. His cock twitched in agreement.

"You *seemed* to be enjoying it. Besides, *you* didn't stop him."

She crossed her arms under her breasts and sank into one hip. The glare in her eyes hadn't wavered. "He's a dragon. How was I supposed to stop him?"

Rainek shrugged. "You could have said no."

His simple comment shocked much of the anger out of her body. She stared at him and felt as if the world around them had gone silent.

Of course she'd said no. She'd told him to stop. Hadn't she? Though it was only a few hours ago, she had a hard time remembering exactly what happened. Except for the orgasms. She remembered those well enough. But surely she'd protested.

She remembered telling him he could kill her and the dragon had laughed but beyond that she couldn't remember if she'd told him to stop or not.

"That's all it would have taken?"

"Probably. I can't say he wouldn't have tried to seduce you into letting him have you, but he wouldn't touch you if you said no." The edge of his mouth pulled up. "Of course, then you'd have a pouting dragon on your hands and that's really annoying."

She felt her mouth sag open. How could he think this was funny? This was a dragon they were dealing with. A ferocious beast that kidnapped and killed countless virgins.

"Tiana, he won't hurt you. And he'd die before he let anything else hurt you."

His tone was serious and flat. It was the same tone he'd used back in the training chamber when he assured her he wouldn't try to escape or seduce her into letting him go. He'd been honest about that. To a point. He'd kept his promise of not escaping "that night" and though he'd seduced her, he hadn't used her to escape.

Instead, he'd touched her body and taught her to crave him. In less than two days, she'd grown addicted to his touch.

"Why does he do it?" she asked, hearing her own voice tremble at the question. "Does he get some kind of pleasure out of it?" She knew the pleasure she'd received but what could the dragon want from licking her sex for hours on end?

Rainek thought about his answer for a moment, then sighed. "Dragons have special needs. The liquid from a woman's..." He hesitated though she knew he'd said the word before. He'd said it to her. He started again. "The liquid from a woman's body is particularly appealing to the dragon. Like a fine nectar. They crave it and it excites them. For a dragon, giving a woman an orgasm with its tongue is equal to his own climax."

"Oh." Tiana didn't know how to respond to that. The dragon liked to lick her because he found pleasure when she found pleasure. That meant he would probably want more. A tingle low in her stomach signaled her body's willingness to accept more of the dragon's loving. "How long have you been collecting women for this dragon?" she asked, shaking herself free of the worrisome thoughts and curious how many women before her had fallen for his rough, desperate lovemaking—and how many had been given to the dragon.

"You're the first he's shown an interest in." He said it so casually as if dealing with a dragon was not a strange occurrence.

He stood up and offered her more fruit. Her stomach rumbled so she accepted the treat and bit into it.

While she ate, he wrapped his hands around her hips and pulled her forward. The blunt head of his cock pushed against her stomach. Tiana took a deep breath. His palms were warm and soothing as he stroked her skin. He made no move to deepen the caress. As if he just wanted to touch her.

"What about you?" she asked.

He lifted her hand to his mouth and slowly licked the fruit juice from her fingers. "What about me?"

"If I told you no, would you accept it?"

He smiled and sucked one finger into his mouth. He swirled his tongue around the end before answering.

"Yes, but I, too, would try to seduce you out of it."

"And why do I think you'd be even more annoying than a pouting dragon?" Tiana couldn't believe those words had come out of her mouth. She wasn't supposed to be flirting with him.

"I'm much more annoying," he agreed with a grin. He bent his head and placed a kiss on her shoulder, her neck, her jaw. With those light, simple touches, Tiana found herself dropping back under his spell.

"Would you like a bath?" Without waiting for an answer, he led her out of the cave. Stars glittered against the black night.

She quickly scanned the sky—spying for the dragon and trying to determine their location. Eventually, she would have to attempt an escape and she needed some idea of where he'd taken her.

Moonlight bounced off the slow moving river. The river wound off to the right, entering a canyon with tall rock walls. To her right, there was open land. She had a fair idea of where they were. About ten miles away from the Keep, a river and cliff like this stood just beyond the Great Forest, which served as the eastern boundary for the Matriarchy lands. When the time was right, she would know which direction to run. Rainek guided her farther into the canyon, down the riverbank to a small, pool.

He lifted her hands and gently untied the knots, the last remnants of the ropes that he'd bound her with. Rope burns scored her skin and he placed his mouth gently on the marks.

"I'm sorry you were hurt." He transferred his attention to the other wrist and treated it in a like manner. She knew it was just a comfort for children but she found the touch of his mouth really did make her pains feel better. "I was afraid you would leave while I slept."

"And now you're not afraid," she asked, surprised to find her voice.

He flicked his tongue across her wrist and looked into her eyes. "I won't let you go."

It was vow, similar to others she'd heard him say. And so far, he'd proven true to his word.

With a gentle nudge, he pushed her toward to the pool. She expected him to join her but actually found it more unnerving to have him sitting on the rocks, watching her with eager eyes.

She quickly dropped into the cold water, trying to cover herself. Rainek folded his arms over his raised knees and watched her.

"Aren't you going to bathe?"

"I already did."

"Are you just going to sit there and watch me?"

Rainek smiled and nodded. "Yes."

She knelt on the river bottom and scooped some of the sand into her hand. Beneath the water, she scrubbed her arms and legs, rinsing his seed from between her thighs.

But he didn't just sit there...he talked. "When I was young..." Rainek began. Splitting his focus between her and the stars above them, he told her stories of his childhood, seemingly random events designed to make her laugh or smile.

Tiana continued her bath but listened all the same. He was truly a charming man, when he wasn't kidnapping women or allowing them to be used by a dragon. Captivated by the story of when he and his sister had climbed to a dragon's lair to seek treasure, she forgot about her bath.

Rainek looked over at her.

"Are you done?"

She nodded.

"Come out." He stood and held out his hand. She had nothing to cover herself with. Rainek didn't move, didn't turn away. He waited. Finally, she rose from the chilly water and reached out to him. The cold must have subdued the fire in her hands because he didn't flinch as he pulled her up on the rock beside him.

"I didn't bring a towel, so let me dry you."

He gently brushed the water droplets off her skin, running his hand across her breasts, down her stomach and legs, urging her to separate her feet so he could reach between her thighs. Then he stood, his amber eyes glowing in the moonlight.

"I missed one." He bent down and sipped a drop of water from her breast. Slowly, he traced her body, licking and drinking from her skin. Finally, he knelt before her. He opened his mouth and stroked his tongue forward along her wet slit.

Tiana shuddered, her body primed by his seductive treatment. She was dripping from her pussy, and he seemed intent on capturing that liquid as well.

"Rainek," she moaned.

He raised his eyes. "I need more of you." His voice was low and powerful.

He seemed to be asking for her permission and she remembered his words. She could send him away if she simply told him no. Even knowing that was the wise decision to make — for her heart and her growing powers—she couldn't. She wanted him, needed him.

"May I have you, love?"

She nodded. Rainek stood and led her back into the cavern and onto the blanket before settling himself beside her. He stroked his hand down the center of her body, from her neck to her mound, smoothing his fingers across her skin. This touch was different. The desperate fucking was replaced by gentle touches and whispered caresses.

When it finally happened, the slow penetration of his cock was sweet almost gentle as he filled her. "Let me have you," he whispered. Tiana sighed and opened herself up to him.

Chapter Six

Tiana jolted awake, her heart pounding as if she'd been ripped from a terrifying dream. Opening her eyes, she realized it was no nightmare. Reality had become much more fantastic than any dream—long hours spent with Rainek's cock or the dragon's tongue inside her. Her hands burned as a potent reminder. She opened her palms and stared at the tiny blue flame that spun across the surface of her skin. She had no idea how long she'd been asleep but it had done little to ease the fire surging through her body.

On top of that, she was exhausted. Rainek had started off with a slow, sensual loving but after that first time, he'd been fierce and hard, thrusting heavily between her legs until she screamed. And begged him to do more. He'd given her the occasional break to eat and rest but always he was there—stroking, touching, as if the mere connection of their flesh was important to him.

Moving slowly because of her tired muscles, she sat up and scanned the cave. The torch jammed into a crack in the stone still illuminated a small area but the rest was shadows. The fire Rainek had built had died leaving a light chill in the cavern.

The blanket beside her was empty. She was alone. He'd left her. The statement sent a sharp stab into her chest, which she wished was fear but knew was regret. Rainek was gone and the dragon…she stared into the darkness of the cave. Was he there? Hiding in the shadows? She rolled over and dragged herself to stand, using the stone wall to support her wobbly legs. The insides of her thighs ached from being spread for so long. And her muscles shook with exhaustion. She'd taken everything Rainek had given her, countering each thrust.

With a sigh, she brushed the tangled mass of her hair away from her face and peered into the shadows. Silence and darkness greeted her but she could sense him. Waiting for her, just beyond the pale light.

After a deep swallow, hoping her courage would rebound, she pushed away from the wall and took a step forward. She could face this creature. If what Rainek said was true, all she had to do was send him away. Never having thought of herself as particularly brave, Tiana was rather pleased that she was on her feet and at least looking to escape. Unfortunately, the only exit lay somewhere beyond the dragon. Huge talons scraped across the cavern floor. The beast was coming for her.

A newly familiar sound of scales swishing against stone sent tension into her shoulders. Rainek's assurances lost a little of their power.

The dragon was out there. *Waiting for you to awaken, waiting to put his tongue between your legs and lick you.* She pressed her lips together to suppress a groan. Strange that her body would desire the dragon's attentions, but with each baby step forward, she felt her pussy contract with anticipation.

Bright black dragon eyes glowed in the darkness. Tiana began a slow retreat, reversing the tiny steps she'd taken forward. What was she going to do? She had no way to protect herself. This was a *dragon.*

She continued her backward creep, never taking her eyes off the creature in front of her. It crouched low and followed her, step by step. A jagged rock poked her in the back. She slapped her hand against the cave wall. She was trapped. There was no place to go.

He won't hurt you. Rainek's words didn't have the soothing effect they'd had earlier. He'd said that she just had to tell him to stop. That the dragon wouldn't touch her if she told him to stop. Staring at the advancing creature, that didn't seem likely. He was intent on her. Intent on having her.

Her pussy fluttered in anticipation—too many memories of that wicked tongue bringing her to climax. Her body had never known such power—except when Rainek was inside her. Between the two of them, she'd discovered her powers and felt them grow.

The dragon stepped forward, standing at the edge of the light. The animal filled half of the cavern but its long neck craned across the room.

Delicious. The wicked tongue flicked out of its mouth. *My turn for more of you.*

She shook her head—rejecting his voice inside her head. Surely this time he would kill her. It didn't matter what Rainek had said—this wasn't Rainek. This was a huge purple and blue beast that was licking its chops like she was its favorite meal. Well, according to Rainek—she was its favorite meal.

Her palms warmed. And Tiana gasped. She had a way to defend herself.

Tiana allowed her gaze to swing past the dragon. There was no one here to witness the use of her power. And she had to protect herself. The dragon waited, still a good distance away.

A twinge of conscience dragged on her. She didn't want to actually hurt the creature. It had once been human and if what Rainek had said was true, the dragon was just doing what its instincts told it. She stretched out one hand, directing her palm up. Taking a deep breath, she willed the fire to flow freely. Heat filled her body as she directed the energy to her hands. Flames exploded from her palm, shattering against the stone ceiling above the animal's head. Hot embers scattered and sparks dropped, falling in an orange shower onto the dragon's snout.

The dragon flinched, jerking its head back, twitching as if something strange had flown up its nose. It stared up at the ceiling then looked curiously at her. Tiana froze. She'd done it. She'd used her power against another being. The guilt that tried to insert itself into her head faded when she realized the beast hadn't moved. It didn't appear to be the least bit frightened. In fact, she thought she saw laughter dancing in the black eyes.

Tiana shook her head. She was imagining things—giving the creature too much credit for understanding. It was just an animal. But there was a strange intelligence in its gaze that worried her.

The embers burned out and Tiana's eyes quickly readjusted to the almost dark cave. She could still see the outline of the creature, see his form well enough to know he wasn't running away as she'd hoped.

The giant dragon head pulled back, then snapped forward. The huge jaws opened and fire burst from the back of his throat and flooded over her. She screamed and crouched down, covering her head as the flames engulfed her. Tiana tensed, waiting, expecting, anticipating the searing of her flesh, the pain.

Warmth flickered across her skin, like tiny fingers.

She lifted her head and stared at her skin. The fire dropped harmlessly to the ground and the air around her cooled. She was unharmed. The dragon's fire hadn't burned her. She held her arm forward, inspecting it. She'd felt the flames bounce against her skin—why wasn't she burned? She looked up at the dragon. He still stood before her—his eyes glittering.

Before she let herself think better of it, she jumped to her feet and flung her hand forward. This time, she directed the flames at the dragon's massive chest. The fire swarmed over him, then trickled to the ground leaving behind a puff of smoke that floated up. When it cleared, Tiana could see a faint burn mark on the dragon's skin. The dragon looked down at his chest then up at her. Again, curiosity and intelligence filled his gaze.

A low growl that sound almost like laughter rumbled from the beast's throat and seconds later another burst of flame covered her. She flinched back. The heat was stronger this time but still not burning. Then she smelled something strange. Burning hair. She looked down and the tips of her blonde hair were black. The creature had set her hair on fire! She slapped at the sizzling ends, quickly smothering the flames.

His quiet chuckle echoed through the cavern. And snapped Tiana's control. She held up both hands and blasted the dragon with every bit of fire left in her body. The flames shot forth, lighting the room, illuminating the surprise on the dragon's face as the fire slammed into this chest. The creature fell back two steps. Tiana followed him, staring intently as she willed the flames from her hands. Power flowed through her veins. She was strong and dangerous.

A gurgle of laughter burst from her throat.

A growl greeted her from behind the wall of flames and Tiana knew she would succeed. She wouldn't stop. She would defeat the dragon who...

The stream of fire pouring from her palms turned thin and began to sink. The flames drooped and fell—like water from a hose that had been turned off—until nothing but tiny sparks dribbled from her fingers.

She flipped her hands around and looked at her palms. The fire was gone, the heat fading.

The dragon crept forward—its black eyes glowing with an eerie fire. Before she could scream, there was another burst of fire. The wall of flames curved around her, herding her toward the wall. She scuttled back until she could go no further. The dragon's flames grew closer, hotter.

"Rainek said you wouldn't hurt me!" she cried over the loud crackling.

The fire evaporated and she found herself face to face with the dragon.

No hurt. Pleasure. Won the game. Want my prize.

Prize? What did he mean "prize"? His long tongue flicked out, whipping across the tip of her breast. As the sweet jolt of pleasure spiraled from her nipple to her clit, she understood. *She* was the prize. Or more precisely, her pussy was the prize. She'd failed in her escape and he wanted her again—wanted to rub that long wet tongue across her body, licking her moisture, enticing more to flow. Her rapid heartbeat flooded her body, making her feel full and ripe.

One last cautious thought told her to flee. She glanced toward the entrance but the path was almost fully blocked by the dragon's body. She would never make it past him. And truth be told, she *had* lost the fight, and that required a surrender of some sort, didn't it? It was appropriate for a gentlewoman to give the champion his boon, she justified silently, ignoring the snickering of her own conscience.

His tongue whispered up the inside of her thigh as if asking permission to taste her and Tiana allowed herself to sink to the ground.

The dragon didn't back away as she lowered herself to the floor, her back propped up against the rock wall. Sliding underneath the huge head, she settled herself on the blankets Rainek had left. Taking a deep breath, she opened her legs and tried to feel like a sacrifice. The black light in the dragon's eyes glowed and he lowered his head.

The first touches were light, almost soothing as he stroked his tongue over her stomach, up to her breasts. He licked up the full mounds, coming close but not touching the sensitive points. She held her breath, the dragon's mouth so close to her head, her neck. With one quick swipe he could kill her—but that seemed to be the last thing he wanted to do. Instead, he continued the long leisurely caresses, over her breasts, up her neck and teasing the sensitive skin behind her ear.

She gritted her teeth together and vowed to be stoic. She would endure his touch. She would allow him his "prize" because she had indeed lost the fight but she wouldn't enjoy it. She wouldn't give him the satisfaction of her satisfaction.

Rainek had said the dragon found pleasure in the juices of her cunt. If she could keep herself removed, resist the pleasure, perhaps he would turn away from her.

His tongue whipped out and swirled around her nipples. The quick sharp taunts sent warm shudders into her belly. No.

She refused to find pleasure in...he wandered down her stomach to the top of her pussy. Hot and wet he teased the first sensitive inch of her passage. Tiana knew from before how powerful that caress was.

Delicious. My prize.

The appreciative voice filled her head while the wicked tongue tickled her pussy—sensation on top of sensation until she wanted to scream with the need for release. Her body quickly leapt on the feeling—craving the pleasures she knew lay near. She twisted her hips, pumping up to drive the dragon into her, to stop the frustrating teases. He growled and the rumble moved through her body. Fear tried to break through her arousal to warn her that she might be angering the beast but she couldn't resist. She needed more—she needed...

"Please," she whispered.

The black glowing eyes stared at her, brighter than she'd seen before. His tongue still worked her, building the pleasure almost to the point of pain but never giving her what she needed.

"Please. Let me come," she begged. Desperate for release, she widened her thighs, drawing her knees up. "I need you."

The dragon pulled back, lifted his head and howled. Before she had a chance to react, he returned, plunging his tongue deep into her cunt. With every thrust, he flicked the long tip against the inside walls of her passage—deep inside where only he and Rainek had ever reached.

Tiana arched up on her shoulders, countering each thrust with one of her own. A vague whisper in the corner of her mind told her she'd not only lost her distance, she was actively fucking the dragon. It didn't matter. All the mattered was the release that called to her—that the dragon could give her.

"Yes," she groaned. "More." The dragon answered her call and pushed deeper before drawing back and circling the tip of his tongue around her clit, then he moved back inside her. The double stimulation pushed her up, higher, her hips waving in the air, her cunt open to his use.

Mine.

The hum that accompanied the word was just the light touch her body needed. Unable to scream—her breath gone— she whimpered as the release pierced her sex. It wasn't a hard shock but a low rumble, not unlike the dragon's growl, that started in her pussy and rolled through her body building in waves as it shuddered toward her limbs. The almost painful sensations washed up her chest, tightening her nipples, and passing through, until it reached the very tips of her fingers.

The tiny corner of her mind still capable of rational thought realized the dragon had lifted his head, withdrawn his tongue from her pussy but she made no move to close her legs. The dragon might want more of her.

* * * * *

She tightened her legs around the dragon's head and cried out as another climax slammed into her. Her world shifted as if the earth beneath her shook in response to her orgasm. She closed her eyes and collapsed back on the ground. There was nothing more she could do. Exhaustion pulled at her. Pleasure overwhelmed her. She needed rest. She needed peace, but she knew if he returned, she'd accept him. What was happening to her? She'd become the dragon's willing partner. A dragon whore. That's what the world called those women.

Still, lying on the stone floor, gasping, desperate for air, she couldn't make herself regret it.

She'd lost track of time and how many times the creature had made her come. There seemed to be no end to its need—or her desire, she thought with a grimace. It was becoming clear that at any time she could push the dragon away if only she had the strength to do it. The strength to deny her body the incredible pleasure he gave her.

As her heart slowed, she realized the dragon wasn't beginning again. Had he left her? Regret filled her chest. She tried to push it aside, to make herself happy that the creature was finished with her but conjuring up that emotion was impossible when her body was limp from so many delicious climaxes.

She let her eyes creep open unsure of what she would feel if the dragon was gone.

The purple and blue dragon *was* gone but in its place was Rainek, naked kneeling between her spread thighs, his cock long, thick, and hard. A twinge of guilt pricked her conscience. She hadn't thought of him the entire time the dragon had been fucking her. It was almost like she'd betrayed him by allowing the dragon to enjoy her body. And to enjoy its touches as well.

She pushed herself up on her hands.

"Rainek, I—" She didn't get a chance to speak. He leaned forward and kissed her. The desperate drive of his tongue into her mouth conquered her senses and erased her concerns. It seemed impossible, after all the dragon had done, after the multitude of orgasms he'd given her, that she could find desire anywhere but as Rainek wrapped his tongue with hers, she felt a new rush of need.

Cocooned in a world where pleasure commanded, Tiana let herself be lured by the kiss and responded with equal strength, feeling a boldness she never expected of herself. Though she'd taken other lovers—this was different. More powerful, more intense. Even his kiss was different. This was so much more than a casual fucking.

Rainek slid his mouth away, planting kisses along her cheek, her jaw, down her neck.

"Let me have you," he pleaded against her skin. He followed the demand with a pump of his hips. The hard line of his cock pressed the inside of her thigh.

"Yes," she whispered, suddenly desperate for the thick penetration of his cock—so different from the dragon's long thin tongue. Rainek reared up and drove forward, pushing deep into her sex, hard and full. It was tight. His cock was so thick that she stretched around him but the light pain only increased her desire. This was what she needed — him filling her, stroking that hard shaft inside her pussy.

My pussy. The voice filled her head even as Rainek plunged into her sex.

"That's it, baby, take me. All of me."

She wanted to give him all she could. She drew her legs up until her knees were bent near her shoulders. Rainek pulled back, drawing out of her pussy. Tiana whimpered at the loss. He soothed her with nonsense sounds as he took her ankles and crossed them, pressing her feet against his stomach and holding her in a deliciously helpless position. Her knees were spread and pushed against her chest, her cunt lifted and opened.

She stared into his eyes — flickering from amber to black and back again, never losing their heat. He reached down and pressed his cock back into her opening. In one long thrust, he was inside her again. The open position of her sex let him ride her deep, each stroke pressing fully on her clit. New shivers went through her cunt every time he filled her. She clutched at his upper arms, needing to hold him, to claim him as the stable part of her world. Her nails bit into his skin. He jerked — as if someone had struck him with fire.

Tiana snatched her hands away — the reality of her curse coming back to her. She'd forgotten. She couldn't touch him. She hadn't worried about the dragon — he seemed immune to fire-- but Rainek's human skin would easily burn. She couldn't bear the thought of hurting him.

Rainek clenched his teeth as she pulled her hands away. Damn it. He wanted to feel her clinging to him, needing him. But it was as if she couldn't bear to touch him. Pain stabbed at his heart. She'd accepted Denith's loving and she seemed to welcome Rainek's fucking but she held herself separate, even distant. He pushed into her, using the soft feel of her cunt wrapped around his cock to distract him from the fear that she wouldn't accept him.

And the dragon.

Now the shivers were real. Like the dragon, Rainek hadn't been content with having her once. After that first climax, he'd pulled out of her and she'd thought he would roll away. Instead, he'd teased her body with seductive caresses until she was begging him to come back inside her. And he had. She had the aches to prove it.

How did this happen? In the short space of two days she'd gone from being a witch with no power to having one of the most dangerous powers around; she'd defied a direct order from the Ruling Family and had allowed a prince and a dragon to fuck her. Hysteria threatened and only the thought that her cries would wake Rainek and forbid her escape allowed her to suppress it. Her hands hummed with warmth. That reminder strengthened her resolve. And the fact that it could become easy — too easy — to become a woman obsessed with the dragon's loving. And Rainek's.

She wouldn't become one of those women. Her life at the Keep wasn't thrilling but it was her own. She wouldn't let herself be at the will of an animal.

A twinge of regret filled her heart at leaving Rainek. He was fascinating and he seemed interested in her. He certainly seemed to enjoy mounting her. Almost as much as the dragon did. It was strange that of all the men who'd been brought to the Matriarchy's lands, he was the one who tempted her — the one who'd inspired enough passion in her to call forth her power with the mere touch of his mouth. Her firefight with the dragon had eased the pain for a while but the climaxes had made it return.

Not that her fire had hurt the dragon. At all. It had thought they were playing. Competing. And she was the prize. She pressed her thighs together, trying to banish the new warmth. It only made it worse. She had to get out, while her sanity — and at least some of her dignity — remained.

She worked first on Rainek's arm, peeling it away from her skin and bending it gently so that it lay between their bodies.

She had to move slowly. If she woke him now, he'd be on her before she reached the entrance to the cave. *And this would be bad, why?* her easily seduced body asked. Unfortunately, she didn't have a good answer. Not one that would satisfy the sensual side of her.

Her upper body free of his hold, she sat up and used her arms to pull her hips back, hoping she could slide out from underneath his leg. The delicious brushes of skin on skin weakened her resolve. So did the massive cock that stretched from his body. *One more time.* She licked her lips and stared at the shaft, imagining it thickening before her eyes.

She could have him one more time—inside her, riding her. And then the dragon, he would return and take over—fucking her with that limber tongue.

Her fingernails bit into the blanket as she physically fought the need to reach out and stroke him.

Focusing on the practical, she continued to slither out of his hold, wiggling her hips up and back, doing her best not to drag the blanket with her as she squirmed.

She was almost free—her knees lying where her hips had been—when she noticed it. His cock, growing, swelling and stretching. She risked a glance at his face but he was still asleep. He was getting hard—even in sleep. She didn't know if it had anything to do with her or if it was the remaining traces of the *reconi* juice but either way, it was tempting.

Her fingers twitched with the physical memory of stroking his thick shaft. She'd touched him that evening in the chamber— but not since. She wanted to feel him, but she couldn't risk it-- couldn't risk wounding that magnificent cock with a casual caress.

She didn't allow herself to dwell on it. She pulled one leg clear of the body cage Rainek had created, then rolled her hips to the side and began to extract her second leg. The tip of her toe raked in the inside of his thigh.

Tiana froze. She held her breath. Rainek was still relaxed in sleep but now there was a hint of a smile on his lips. Heat curled inside her stomach as she wondered what—or who—he was dreaming about. As she watched, he rolled onto his back. His now hard cock sprung up, stretching toward his stomach. A low ache melted the center of her body. It would be so easy to mount him, ride him the way a male should be ridden. She could almost feel it, imagine kneeling above him, pumping her ass up and down, letting that delicious cock touch her as she decreed it. She licked her lips, which had gone dry from her heavy breaths. It was tempting. He was tempting.

Blue fire burst from her right hand. The flame fell harmlessly against the rock but served as the warning she needed. Rainek and his orgasms had caused this fire in her body. If she stayed away from him, perhaps they would subside and she could return to her old life.

First, she had to get back to the Keep. Merena was going to be furious that her captive had escaped but at least Rainek would be free of whatever plot she'd concocted for him. There had to be a particular reason that Merena had chosen Rainek. Why else would she have risked kidnapping a prince from such a powerful kingdom?

Suddenly finding herself free—and a little chilled at the loss of Rainek's warmth—Tiana stood, her muscles stiff and aching from the stone bed. Her shirt was draped over a rock in the corner. None of her other clothes had come with her. Rainek had stripped off her overdress before fucking her against the wall back at the Keep. The long cotton shirt hung down to the tops of her thighs, giving her at least some cover. She tightened the laces at the bodice trying to ignore the memories of Rainek's hands ripping those same ties.

The ropes he'd used to tie her hung on the cave wall. She briefly considered tying him up but decided against it. There was the risk of waking him while she was doing it—and she'd seen the destruction of the training chamber. If he could pull chains from a stone wall, he would have no problem ripping rope to shreds.

It was time. Nothing was holding her back...except the enticing prospect of Rainek waking and finding her. Innate honesty compelled her to admit that she was stalling, almost hoping he would capture her again.

Bowing once again to staid wisdom, she started toward the entrance. Her feet slowed as she reached the door. One last look. What could it hurt?

His form was still relaxed, the contented sleep of a well-sated lion.

"Good-bye, Rainek," she whispered

Long shadows created by the afternoon light reached into the cave making the entrance dark. She stepped into the edge of the sunlight, inching along the wall, trying to locate the dragon. Was he waiting out there? Guarding while Rainek took his turn with her. She wanted that to sound more sinister than it truly was. Rainek had been wonderful, a powerful lover who seemed to enjoy giving her pleasure. She hadn't minded at all not being on top.

She took another step. She was outside the Matriarchy lands and therefore outside their protection. There were bandits in these areas who patrolled the Matriarchy border searching for wayward women. Once they left the Matriarchy's borders, the queen felt little compulsion to protect her subjects.

Of course, what's the likelihood that a group of bandits would be in this particular area? Tiana asked silently, trying to convince herself that she would be safe if she went out there.

Tiana took a deep breath and moved away from the rocks. It was quiet. No mental cry, no voice called for her to stop. No rustle of dragon wings.

She looked across the low river that ran outside the cavern. In the far distance was the start of the forest that designated her queen's lands. The trees would give her protection. Given the size of the dragon, he wouldn't be able to fly or chase her once she was within the forest. The sun was sinking quickly. She had about an hour until full darkness. She couldn't be in the open after dark. If rumors were true—and so far they'd been remarkably accurate—a dragon's night vision was particularly strong.

But there was nothing between her location and the edge of the forest. That meant running across an open plain, made up of hard soil and little vegetation. It also meant she had to move fast...and speed had never been her strong point.

Drawing in a lungful of air, she took off, galloping through the river. The icy water splashed up her thighs cooling her overheated skin—and inciting her overheated senses. She considered stopping and washing off the evidence of Rainek's lovemaking but knew she didn't have the time. Rainek would awaken soon and the dragon could be returning. She couldn't be anywhere near when that happened.

Her short legs carried her in clumsy steps across the plain. She'd spent her adult life managing the Keep. Now, she wished she'd joined Sierra and her guards on a few of those longer hikes. She'd watched the warriors train and wished she had their endurance.

The gentle aches between her thighs from Rainek's heavy thrusting worked themselves out as she ran. She allowed herself occasional glances behind her to see if the dragon was chasing her but there was nothing. She was alone.

Already exhausted before she'd even started, she quickly tired. Rainek and the dragon had fucked the strength from her legs. She felt herself slowing as the sun began to sink below the horizon. She was less than halfway there. The dark mass of the Great Forest was within sight but she would never make it before sundown.

Her only hope was that the dragon didn't notice she was gone.

She listened for the sound of dragon wings floating on the air. Instead, the thunder of hooves across the arid ground reached her, making the hair on the back of her neck stand up. *Not a dragon.*

Bandits. She didn't stop running, panic giving new strength to her legs. If they caught her before she reached the forest, she was going to wish the dragon had found her first. She ran but the ground felt like mush beneath her feet. How was she going to escape? Where was the dragon when—

A hemp band flew over her head and fell, closing with a snap around her waist, her arms locked to her side. The rope was jerked, pulling her to stop. Tiana stumbled, her feet still moving as she slammed into the ground. Without her hands to catch her, she twisted and landed on her shoulder. Breath exited her lungs in a rush and she couldn't seem to replace it. Lifting her cheek out of the dirt, she gasped, concentrating on being able to breathe. Finally, the constriction on her chest eased and she realized she was on her stomach with her backside up in the air, no doubt bared to her captors.

Self-preservation and modesty prevailed over fear and she rolled over, ready to face the bandits. She glanced downward to make sure her shirt was covering her sufficiently, then lifted her chin and raised her eyes up to the criminal who'd captured her.

He wore a fine silk jacket that hung down to his boots as he sat on the tooled leather saddle.

He's a little too well-dressed for a bandit.

"Well, it seems we've caught ourselves some live bait."

Chapter Seven

The sneering man in the fancy clothes deliberately moved his gaze down her body, lingering on her legs. The white shirt didn't cover much beyond her crotch.

"*You're* the best the Matriarchy could sacrifice? No wonder the dragon remained behind." His top lip bent upward as he spoke as if she was to blame for something.

Tiana ignored the mockery in his words. She knew she wasn't the prettiest woman in the land but Rainek—and the dragon—seemed to enjoy her. She clung to that strange bit of comfort and raised her chin in defiance. Using a tone she'd heard Merena use many times with those she considered stupid, Tiana said, "I wasn't *sacrificed*. We don't believe in —"

"You went to him willingly?"

"No." His question jolted her out of her faked arrogance. "I was kidnapped," she defended.

"Even better. The dragon chose you. He'll want you back," he announced.

"He won't. I was just a convenient hostage." And a convenient fuck—for both of them. She glanced back the way she came, looking for some sign of the dragon. Dragons were notoriously vicious to men. Not that she hoped for leniency for her newest set of kidnappers but it seemed unwise to irritate a dragon. "The queen will pay well for my return."

"Oh, we'll return you without ransom."

A second horseman rode forward. He stared down at her as well and the same look of disgust marked his face. Tiana did her best not to cringe in front of the huge angry man. Instead, she kept her chin raised. She wouldn't cower before criminals.

"Yes," the new arrival agreed. "Why would we want a dragon whore in our lands? Our women are pure. They don't need to be infected by lust."

Two things struck Tiana at once—she had been trying to escape so she didn't think she qualified as a "dragon whore" and these men thought lust in a woman was something nasty. His bigotry gave her strength. She couldn't wait to be returned to the Keep. Or the dragon. Anything was better than this.

"What are you going to do with me?" Anger—irritation really—gave her strength to show some of the defiance she hid from her own people.

The second arrival climbed off his horse and took another length of rope. Without a word, he loosened the main knot around her waist enough to free her hands then pulled them behind her. The tight strands cut into her already tender wrists. Her chest pushed forward, her full breasts pressing against the fabric of her shirt.

The first man stared at her and an evil smirk curled his mouth.

"Maybe I *can* understand why the dragon chose you. You've got a nice set of tits on you."

Her second captor slipped one hand up and squeezed her breast.

"Nice and firm, too, Gaynor." His voice sent a shiver of disgust across her skin and Tiana couldn't hide her reaction. She leaned away, trying to escape his touch. "What, bitch, you'd rather have that creature fuck you than a real man?"

Tiana pressed her lips together and turned her head away. She could never explain, and they would never understand, that the dragon had been more of a gentleman to her than they ever would. Having encountered these men, she knew that Rainek's words were true. She could have stopped the dragon by simply saying no.

"Leave her be, Maris," Gaynor commanded. "She's bait. If there is anything left after we've killed the dragon, we'll each have a turn with her. They don't care for another's scent on their whores." He spoke with such viciousness that Tiana's stomach flipped over.

Maris tugged the rope around her waist tight then pulled. Tiana had to stumble to standing or risk being dragged across the ground. He walked the end of the rope over to Gaynor and handed him the length.

"I'll let you ride with me," Gaynor announced, staring down hard at Tiana. "But don't think you'll seduce me into letting you go. I'm immune to your slut charms."

Tiana felt her jaw drop open. "I was trying to get away from him, in case you didn't notice."

The words were strong and a little sarcastic. Tiana didn't know where they'd come from but she suspected it was from the experience of having a prince kidnap her and a dragon fuck her. She'd gotten mouthy during the whole process. Besides, what did she have to lose? These cretins were going to use her as "bait" no matter what. They didn't deserve common courtesy.

Gaynor's lips tightened and his nostrils spread wide as if he smelled something vile in her general direction.

"It doesn't matter. You let him touch you."

"Let him?" The words came out of her mouth in a squeak. True, she *had* let him, encouraged him even, but somehow telling that to her captors didn't seem wise.

He continued as if she hadn't spoken. "Better that you would have died than to submit to the touch of that creature."

Tiana nodded. Not agreeing but realizing there was nothing more to say to this man. And thanking the Goddesses that she'd never be married to a man like this. She could only imagine the marriage bed for his wife. Eyes closed, enduring the quick pumping until he could spill his seed.

Now Rainek—*that* man knew how to make it pleasurable for his lover.

And she'd left him. Standing here—captured and bound by bandits—escaping from Rainek seemed like a pretty bad idea. At least she knew what to expect from him.

Finally, Gaynor pulled her forward. With a quick flip of his wrist, he tightened the rope around her waist until she couldn't breathe. In one awkward movement he bent down, heaved her up, and draped her across the saddle. The flaps of her shirt fluttered around her backside and she knew she was bare-assed to the world. Gaynor loosened the rope, easing the pressure on her chest but with her arms tied behind her, she had no way to stabilize herself. Every step of the horse rocked her body. Her new captor clicked his heels and the horse lunged forward.

"Could I have something to cover me?" she asked, turning her head and looking up. And hoping they weren't going far. This was an uncomfortable position to be in.

"No. The dragon will be lured by your whore scent and will follow."

She sagged forward and let the bounce of the horse knock the frustration out of her before she tried again.

"Where are you from?" she asked curious about the well-dressed dragon hunters.

The man hesitated as if he wasn't going to answer, then he spoke. "I am Gaynor, head of the Council in Wranne."

She recognized the name of the town as one near the Matriarchy borders. The town was led by a male council who didn't approve of the Matriarchy and refused to do business with women. Tiana sighed. They didn't allow their women much freedom but at least now she knew who she was dealing with.

"So, has this dragon done a lot of damage?" She had no idea where the dragon had gone while Rainek was inside her.

Gaynor grunted, then said, "No. This is the first we've seen of the beast in our area."

She pulled her head up and stared over her shoulder at him. "Then why are you going after it if it's never done anything to you?"

"It's a dragon. Dragons are the demon's spawn. They kill our livestock, torch our homes and turn our women into sluts."

It was a view commonly held. And Tiana couldn't say she'd never heard of a nice, domesticated dragon but it seemed unfair to attack a creature before it had done anything wrong.

It hadn't killed her when it had the chance. *No, it was too busy putting its tongue between your legs to think about killing you.*

And turning our women into sluts. The statement swirled through her head. Was that what had happened to her? It seemed like an overstatement. She didn't *feel* like a slut. She'd enjoyed what the dragon had done to her, she was willing to admit that, but that didn't make her a slut. She had no desire to fuck any of the men currently around her.

They rode for another hour. The sun was fully set when they stopped. Tiana scanned the sky as she was lifted off the horse. If the dragon was going to come after her, he would be able to see in the dark.

But if he was going to come after her, where in the Hells was he?

Gaynor ordered her bound to a rock—her arms chained above her and her legs spread wide. She was allowed to keep her shirt on, to avoid "tempting" her captors. She rolled her eyes at that comment and settled down to wait. It wasn't a particularly comfortable rock but at least it wasn't a horse and she knew one of two things would happen. Either she would be left lying there until morning when hopefully her captors would realize the dragon had gone on to another woman and she would be freed. Or the dragon would come for her...and she hadn't quite decided how that scenario ended.

The men who traveled with Gaynor ducked down behind the rocks that surrounded her stage. With a caution not to warn her dragon "lover", Gaynor joined his men.

She wanted to protest that the dragon wouldn't come after her—that she'd been convenient—but she held her voice. The dragon seemed possessive of her. She couldn't stop the shudder that ran down her back. His voice in her head—asking for more. Declaring that she was his. *Mine.* She'd never had one word fill her with such emotion—fear and anticipation. Lust.

No, if the dragon did find them, she had no doubt that he would take care of her attackers.

And then he would turn to her.

* * * * *

Rainek eased his hand down his side and curled his palm and fingers around his hardened cock. *Tiana.* He wanted to dream about her a little longer. She'd been so sweet, so perfect for him.

He didn't open his eyes, knowing he would be sorely disappointed if he awoke in his own bed—if this had been an elaborate dream created by Denith.

Mine?

At Denith's question, Rainek opened his eyes. Denith would have sensed her if she were nearby. He looked at the space beside him. Empty. The quiet of the cavern warned him she was *truly* gone.

"Hells, she's escaped."

Leave us?

Again the wild dragon panic flooded Denith's usually logical voice.

Rainek tried to calm the frantic beast but the dragon's pain moved through him. He had to find her. *Find her.*

He had no idea how long she'd been gone or where she'd headed but she was out there somewhere. Rainek stepped into the rising moonlight and took a deep breath. Denith immediately recognized her scent and urged him on. Rainek stopped the dragon's intent, holding them in place.

"Wait. Let's think about this."

Mine. Want mine, was Denith's only response.

"We'll get her. She's not going to get away from us." He stood, silently blaming himself for not keeping better track of her. They were miles away from anything. He stepped outside. Where could she have gone?

Denith focused his senses, gathering the distinct flavor of Tiana across the air. Rainek recognized her particular fragrance—the delicious perfume of her cunt—then noticed that others blended with Tiana's. Male scents.

Before he could blink, the dragon took over—consuming his awareness and exploding into his full corporeal form.

The transition was always a shock for Rainek, a jolt as his body disappeared and the dragon formed. And the strange sensation that when this happened, he was the rider in another's mind, present, but not in control.

Quickly Denith picked up her trail. The path was faint but the mix of Tiana—with a trace of Rainek's scent still on her—led him skyward. With a scream that vibrated the flowing water, Denith leapt into the air and streaked toward the dense forests.

Her fragrance grew stronger as the dragon sped along. Then Rainek noticed a change. The wet smell of her sex changed from seduction to fear. Denith flew faster, needing his mate, needing to capture her and taste her.

Her path was a straight line, headed toward the Grand Forest, then it veered north. Denith turned with it. The trail grew stronger as he chased them—men and horses. And Tiana. Rainek couldn't think clearly enough. Denith's passion barreled through his thoughts whenever he tried to reason through the situation. Had Tiana gone with them willingly?

Mine! The furious dragon shouted, denying the very possibility and mentally knocking Rainek back.

A weak light—fire—caught his attention. Denith sped up, thinking only of claiming his mate.

Seeing through the dragon's eyes was different from human vision. Colors were different—muted—but the lines were distinct and explicit. Tiana's white blouse glowed like a star against the dark stone. The pale light from her flesh revealed her spread out position.

Denith released another bone-cracking scream and dived down. Rainek did nothing to slow the creature. If they had touched Tiana, Rainek would destroy them.

If there was anything left when Denith was finished.

* * * * *

Stretched out as she was—and filled with thoughts of what might happen—it was impossible for her to relax. She tugged on the ropes. *By the Goddesses, I've spent a lot of time in this position during the last two days.* She stared at her hands willing them to heat and burn through the fibers but there was nothing. Exhaustion seemed to have drained the fire from her system. And after all the pleasuring she'd received from Rainek and the dragon, that was saying something.

She didn't know how long she laid there—her legs open, her captors watching from their hiding places.

Then, she heard it—the heavy rush of wings. Big wings. Dragon wings. And a scream that shook the ropes that bound her.

The creature was black against the night sky, plunging toward the outcropping of rocks. She swallowed deeply, gulping in air to sustain her when no doubt the breath would be frightened out of her. The fierce cry repeated as he swept down, landing on the rocks below her legs.

The dragon didn't look around. A furious light glowed in his black eyes as he stared at her.

Touch you?

It took a moment for the meaning of his question to sink in but she knew immediately what would happen to the men if she said yes. The dragon would torch them all.

"Watch out, they—" She never go a chance to finish her warning. The first man attacked, driving a long spear into the dragon's side. The dragon screamed and whipped around snapping at the man. Others poured out of their hiding places between the rocks—swords and daggers glittering in the bright moonlight.

They moved at him in coordinated waves—attacking and retreating, only to have the other side attack. The dragon whipped his tail around, knocking three men hard into the rocks, but it wasn't enough. There were too many of them—stabbing and piercing his hard skin. Blood began to flow from the myriad of wounds on his side.

Tiana pulled on the ropes that held her. She couldn't stand to watch this. They were killing him.

Heat flared in her hands. Fear hadn't been enough. It had taken anger. As the fire flowed through her body, she gripped the ropes and released the sudden jolt of heat in her palms. The hemp shredded beneath the flames. She tore at the bonds around her ankles and lunged to her feet. She didn't stop to think, didn't stop to consider her secret. She opened her palms and blasted the nearest man with all the anger and fury inside her.

The flames burst forth and knocked him backward, slamming him into the rocks. He crumpled to the ground, his eyes falling shut.

"She's a fire witch!" The cry went out. Tiana ignored it and sent another blast of fire toward the men hacking at the dragon's left side. Her flames washed over them and their shouts filled the night. She watched as they retreated, slapping at the fire and sparks igniting their leathers and silks.

The dragon took advantage and spun around to face the other group. With a quick slash of his huge head, he sent them flying. Bodies fell with deadly thumps on the granite. He opened his mouth and enveloped them in flames. Tiana stalked forward, her hair caught by the night wind, swirling in wild strands around her face.

A foreign energy welled up inside her. She was strong and powerful. A warrior goddess protecting her lover. She followed the men as they ran, sending jolts of fire after them, herding them toward their retreat. As if the fire inside her was unlimited, she sent wave after wave of flame—finding vindication in their shouts of pain. The fancy leather and silk clothes burned quickly. She was careful to direct her fire toward their leathers but she knew some of them would be singed.

She chased them across the rocks until they dropped their swords and fled. She stood and watched the darkness, until the night was quiet. She spun around and returned to the clearing.

She approached cautiously, not knowing who was left. The dragon stood alone. Bodies lay in crumpled piles at the edges of the rocks. Some were clearly breathing. Others were not.

As she climbed down the rock, the dragon laboriously swung his head around to face her.

Mine.

The voice was different this time. Softer, weaker.

Touch you?

Though his voice was whispery thin, she knew the answer was important. "No. Just to bring me here." She shook her head to accompany her words. "They didn't hurt me." A thin wedge of anger erupted in the dragon's eyes. "Or pleasure me," she quickly added. Her captors had been punished enough. Somehow the dragon's potential reprimand seemed too harsh. She would let the queen deal with the marauders once she returned to the Keep.

Mine?

The question was a mere hiss as the dragon sank to the ground. Tiana gasped as he collapsed, the huge spear protruding from his side. Reddish-black blood, illuminated by moonlight, flowed freely from the wounds along his side and neck.

"Oh, no. Dragon?"

Denith.

She shook her head, not understanding.

"What's Denith?"

Me. Denith.

"Denith? Is that your name?" she asked, feeling responsible for this magnificent creature's death.

Yes.

"Well, hold on, Denith. We'll figure out something. Just don't die."

The beast didn't answer. The black in his eyes faded and a hint of amber appeared. She'd heard tell that a dragon's eyes changed color but didn't understand the meaning. What was she supposed to do? How was she supposed to heal a dragon? He'd been attacked trying to save her — or retrieve her — either way it was her fault he was hurt.

She knelt down beside his head and stroked her hand across the solid jaw. His scales were smooth beneath her palm.

Mine?

She knew that he meant her so she answered. "Yes, I'm here." She leaned against his neck, feeling his warmth seep into her body. Silence filled the night sky but Tiana didn't move. She lay beside him, her head against his neck, feeling his pulse beat beneath her cheek.

Stay?

"Of course, I'll stay. I won't leave you." She patted her hand on his side, staring at the spear. She had to pull it out. Maybe there was some way to stop the bleeding if she got the weapon out. The other slash marks seeped blood but clearly the most dangerous wound was the deep penetration of the spear.

Amulet.

This word seemed to come from a different source. The voice was clearer and more human. She looked around. The dragon wore no amulet. What did it mean?

"Uh, right. I'm going to pull the spear out and see how bad it is."

Amulet, he whispered again.

She completely ignored him this time and stood. Denith growled as she moved away so she whispered assurances that she wasn't going far. Keeping one hand on his shoulder, to let him know she was near, she climbed over his legs and down to where the spear protruded from his side.

"This might hurt," she warned as she wrapped her hands around the long pole. The strength and energy from before had faded when she'd seen Denith collapse. She needed it now. Calling on exhausted reserves, she pulled with everything she had left. It resisted, scraping the inside of the wound on the way out even as it had on the way in. The dragon screamed but Tiana didn't stop. She had to remove it. Gritting her teeth, she continued her steady pull and finally, the spear came free. Red covered the lower half of the pole.

And new blood gushed from his side.

The dragon began to shimmer. Pain filled the groan that slipped from the animal's throat and then he shrank. The huge bulk before her collapsed down and instantaneously reformed into a human body. Rainek's human body.

Surprise knocked the air out of her. What had just happened? Where had the dragon gone? Her mind raced to adjust. Rainek and the dragon were the same creature? She knew, as everyone did, that dragons were formed by a human being bitten, but she'd never heard of a dragon turning into a human.

Blood continued to flow from the deep stab wound—now in Rainek's side. He was bleeding. Badly. She would figure out how Rainek and Denith were the same creature later. After she'd healed him.

Silver flashed across his chest—silver in the shape of a dragon. An amulet. She didn't know what she was supposed to do with it only that Rainek seemed to think it was important. Maybe it was magic.

Magic existed. She knew that. She was a witch after all. But was there magic strong enough to heal him?

Shifting him to his back, she quickly pulled the amulet off. The dragon form was warm in her palm giving her hope that there was some magic in it. She waved the amulet over the wound. Nothing happened.

Clutching the amulet to her chest, she closed her eyes and begged the Goddesses who protected her to show her how to use it to cure him.

Her world spun for a second and when she opened her eyes, she was staring at a stranger. The man jumped up from his desk and stared hard at her. His eyes flickered with the same intensity of Rainek's.

"Who are you?" he demanded. "Where's Rainek?"

She looked down at the amulet gripped between her palms and saw she was quite see-through. She eased her hold on the dragon medallion and the picture before her wavered. She squeezed the amulet and the image stabilized.

"Where's Rainek?" the gruff man repeated.

"Rainek's hurt. The dragon was attacked."

"Denith was attacked? Where are you?"

She looked around trying to pinpoint their location. "On the south border of the Matriarchy. We need help. Where are you?"

"The castle of Xicanth."

Rainek groaned and flopped his head to the side.

Tiana released the medallion. She understood its power now. It called to Rainek's home but it did her no good. It was too far away. Rainek needed help now.

She slipped the amulet's chain over her neck, the dragon medallion hanging low between her breasts. She would keep it for Rainek and return it to him when he was healed, she vowed, because she was going to help him. He was not going to die because of her.

She pulled off her shirt and wiped the blood away. More took its place almost immediately. The wound was so deep mere pressure wouldn't stop it. She needed something to make the bleeding stop.

Fire.

She opened her palms upward. Flames flickered across her skin. She had a source of fire.

Not knowing if she'd kill him or heal him but knowing she had to try, she knelt beside his hips. His eyes fluttered open but she knew he didn't actually see her. She placed her hands over the large wound left by the spear. Fire danced across her palms. Praying to her Goddesses and the Gods who protected him, for strength and knowledge, she covered the deep hole and released the heat from her hands, letting little streams of flame flow into the wound. The slow release was almost painful as the fire begged to burn free but she held back, moving slowly, circling the edges first. She pulled her hands free to check her progress. Black lined the edge of the tear where she'd burned his flesh. But the bleeding stopped where her fire had touched.

Hoping she wasn't hurting him further, she stuck her fingers into the wound and again released the tiny flames. Working slowly and delicately, she moved through the blood and cauterized the deepest veins.

She lost track of time, knowing only that the moon was rising and her back was straining but she couldn't stop. Finally, after she'd worked each area, she pulled back. Blood covered her hands, his skin, and her shirt but it seemed to have worked. No new blood was appearing.

But there was no way to know if he would survive.

The bone-crushing exhaustion from a day with almost no sleep, followed by being captured and left as bait, not to mention the firefight afterward, dragged on her body and her soul. She wanted nothing more than to sleep. Every bit of strength had been wrung from her body. But she forced herself to keep going. She checked his other wounds, left by the men's swords and daggers, and ran a light flame over many of them.

Denith's strong hide had been able to deflect most of the blades, she thought with some satisfaction.

Finally finished, she sat on the ground and stared blankly at the man beside her.

The threat was gone and Rainek was as healed as she could make him. Her tired mind flipped through all that had happened and the revelation that still stunned her—that Rainek was able to turn from human to dragon and back again. That the creature who'd spent so long with his tongue between her legs and the man who liked to fuck her were the same being.

A light breeze sent shivers up her arms. Seeing that Rainek was asleep, she gathered the remaining wood that her captors had collected to feed the signal fire. After dragging it over beside Rainek, she stacked the logs and smiled as she held out her hand. Flames instantly flowed from her palm, just enough to light the twigs she'd placed at the base. Soon the fire burned cheerfully with the rocks and the night behind it.

I'm starting to like this power, she thought as she settled herself behind Rainek. Keeping his front to the fire, she curled around his back, wrapped her arms around his chest and held him. The heat from her body flowed into his and she cuddled him close.

She forced herself to remain awake. The men who'd fled—either from her fire or Denith's—might gather reinforcements and decide to return.

In the late hours of the night, one of the wounded—left behind by his comrades—awoke, his groan filling the silent sky. Tiana slipped away from Rainek and stood, ready to protect the man she loved. She stumbled over a nonexistent crack in the rock. Love? She couldn't love him. She barely knew him. He'd kidnapped her and fucked her. He was a prince—with a sweet smile and an obvious love for his family.

The attacker stood, distracting her from the path of her thoughts. He practically ignored Tiana as he scanned the landscape. He was looking for the dragon but, thankfully, didn't seem to see Rainek's body lying on the ground. He finally noticed her, waiting. Vengeance and power crept into the man's gaze as he picked up a dropped sword. He thought she was alone, unprotected—and a dragon whore. He took two steps toward her.

Her initial response was to step back but she held herself steady. She'd faced much worse things in the past two days than a cowardly man who would lay a trap for a magnificent creature like Denith. She straightened her spine and held her hand out, palm flat and facing up. She concentrated on the flame, forcing it to form into a ball.

He fell back, tripping as he moved, recognizing the not-so-subtle warning. Never taking his eyes off her or the fireball that hovered over her hand, he crawled away, turning and running only when he reached the top of the rocks.

Tiana sighed—a combination of relief and irritation. She didn't doubt he would return—along with all his other dragon-killing buddies. They would have to leave as soon as Rainek was awake.

* * * * *

The sun crept over the horizon, easing the chill that had settled into Tiana's bones with its morning warmth. Rainek lay still beside her. As she had throughout the night, she placed her fingers against his neck and sighed in relief as she felt the strong steady pulse. Somehow, he'd survived the night. Still covered in smeared blood, he looked pale but alive.

But with the sun, the men who'd hurt him might return. Tales of a dragon and a fire witch working together no doubt were flying through the town. Now, the townspeople would have double the reason to fear them. They had to get moving.

"Rainek?" She kept her voice soft but pushed his shoulder with the heel of her hand. "Rainek, we need to get going."

His eyelids fluttered but didn't open. She nudged him again and added a little more force to her call.

"Rainek," she said, hoping to push past the pain that kept him locked in his mind.

Again his eyes twitched but his time, the lids rose and he stared up at her. For a moment, the amber depths were cloudy and confused as if he was still dreaming. Then his eyes cleared.

"Tiana." He reached out of her. The sharp movement made him wince.

"Don't move. You're hurt."

He groaned and grimaced in one painful movement. "I can tell. What happened?"

"You were stabbed. Or actually, Denith was stabbed."

Rainek placed his hand over the deep stab wound.

"You know about Denith?" His voice was tense and shaky.

She nodded then she watched his eyes turn vacant as if he was listening to a voice she couldn't hear. She realized he was hearing the dragon.

"Do you remember what happened?" she asked.

Rainek shook his head. "Not much. I remember Denith landing and then all the Hells came to life." He drew in a shallow breath. "I remember fire. Lots of fire." Tiana nodded but didn't say anything. "Denith was completely in charge. Most of it's pretty hazy." He looked at the wound on his side. A fresh trickle of blood began to flow.

She gasped and reached forward. He waved her away. "It will be fine. Denith heals quickly."

His body tensed and she knew he was preparing to stand.

"We'd better go," he moaned. "Those men will probably be back to see what's left of the dragon and neither of us is in any shape to fight them off."

She scrambled to her feet and reached down to help Rainek. Again, he waved her away and then asked her to step back. Way back. A little hurt that he rejected her assistance, she did as he asked and walked backwards until he nodded that she could stop. Then before her eyes, he disappeared. There was a shimmer and a flash, and Denith stood before her, his scales glittering purple and blue in the morning sunlight.

A slash of red still stained his side but she could see the wound was healing on the giant beast.

The dragon stared down at her, his tongue slipping out and licking the side of his mouth. It was too easy to remember the feel of him in her pussy, curled around her clit. Even exhaustion didn't eliminate the response in her body—her sex relaxing and turning damp, her knees trembling.

The black glow of Denith's eyes brightened as if he could sense her arousal. Red crept up her cheeks but before she could sink into total embarrassment, Denith stepped forward. Despite knowing that this was Rainek—somewhere deep inside—she had to will herself not to move. It would take some getting used to a dragon casually approaching her.

Denith bent forward, licking up the inside of her knee, and higher, along her thigh and then just to the tip of her pussy. With a quick swipe as if to tease himself with her flavor, he slid his tongue along her slit then pulled away.

Delicious. Need you.

She didn't get a chance to respond as he sat on his haunches, and reached for her with his massive front claws. Her body instinctively tensed up, preparing to be ripped by his sharp talons. She closed her eyes and waited but no pain followed. Warm, soft pads circled her. She felt her feet leave the ground. He pulled her close, cradling her against his chest, his touch gentle. She opened her eyes but could see nothing except the dark purple of his chest. His muscles tightened and expanded and he leapt into the air. The steady pulse of his wings beat in time with her heart, soothing her as the cold air rushed by. Shivering slightly, she snuggled into Denith's warmth, clinging to the dragon as he flew.

She should have been terrified but she knew she was safe. Denith held her in his arms and he wouldn't let her go.

The finality of that statement prodded her tired mind but she ignored it, knowing she would have to deal with reality later. That Rainek, even if he was part dragon, was a prince and would require a wife like Merena. And that dragons were notorious for using women for short periods of time then killing or rejecting them. Her time with Rainek and Denith was short. If the dragon didn't reject her, then Merena would take Rainek away. Even knowing she was putting her heart at risk, Tiana made the rash decision to enjoy it. She rubbed her cheek against the strong chest and heard a deep rumble from beneath her ear.

She snuggled up to the beast, drifting into a light sleep with the comforting rhythm of his heart beneath her ear, waking only when his powerful legs eased them to the ground. She blinked and raised her head. They were back by the river. Denith lowered her down.

She reached out, trying to find the ground with her hand before she hit it, but instead she sank into icy water.

"Ahh!" She didn't have a chance to stop the dragon as he released her. The cold shot through her body as her backside landed on a large smooth rock on the river bottom. Gasping for air, trying to counteract the shock, she stared up. Denith tilted his head to the side as if confused by her reaction.

Dragons obviously react differently to cold, she thought.

Wash?

She nodded and shivered at the same time. A bath sounded wonderful but she didn't remember the water being this cold when Rainek had let her bathe the day before. Denith backed away, finding a deeper place in the river. She watched in fascination as the dragon rolled and twisted in the clear water.

Tiana sat up straight, her breasts resting on top of the water. A shiver assailed her as a fresh rush of water teased her nipples.

The dragon might be content with freezing water but she wasn't.

She stared at the slow eddy the dragon had placed her in. Maybe she could heat it up. She slapped her hand just beneath the surface and released some of the heat. Warmth welled up and flowed around her. Moving quickly, she gathered some sand from the river bottom and began to scrub her skin. She had to reheat the pool three times before she was completely satisfied with her bath but finally she stood and let the water drip from her skin. Sun caressed her as she dropped her head back, welcoming the morning warmth into her body.

When she opened her eyes, Denith was there. Lust erupted from his gaze and Tiana knew what he needed without being told. Moving to the rocks that lined the river, she sat down, rolling to her back and opening her legs, presenting her naked sex to him.

Denith growled softly, a sound she heard echoed in her pussy, and leaned forward. A deliberate swipe of the dragon's tongue swept across her thigh and the tip of her sex.

That's my pretty mate. So delicious. So hungry for me.

The dragon lowered his head and pushed his tongue into her passage. The orgasm that shot through her body was impossible to contain. She screamed as he thrust into her. The sound was pure pleasure. Her body thrummed with the feeling—like sparklers from the center of her cunt fluttering out through her blood until it was too much for her body to contain.

Mine.

Tiana heard the voice in her head even as her body accepted the hungry passion that was thrust upon her. She gave the only answer that she could.

"Yes."

Mine, he repeated and returned with intensity to her cunt. With nothing to cling to, she placed her hands on the dragon's head and let him take her.

* * * * *

Tiana collapsed down, her back rubbing against the river stone. Denith plunged his tongue into her jolting her to another climax, until her body was screaming from too much pleasure. Every teasing stroke sent a new wave of shivers through her body. There was nothing left to offer him. He'd taken it all.

"Tiana?"

Her eyes fluttered open. Rainek knelt beside her.

"Denith?" she asked, not knowing where the dragon went when Rainek appeared. Rainek grimaced slightly.

"He's gone. For now."

Too exhausted from the constant pressure in her sex to do anymore but nod, she did so and then sighed as Rainek lifted her into his arms, holding her safely against his chest. She curled into his warmth and smiled. It reminded her of the dragon's heat.

Even with her eyes closed she noticed when the sunlight disappeared and darkness once again surrounded them. He put her down and she felt the familiar roughness of the wool blanket. They were back in the cave.

She smiled up at him, ready for sleep but Rainek shook his head. He cupped her cheek in his huge hand and forced her to look at him.

"Can you stay awake for a few minutes? Let me get you some water and something to eat." His fingers skipped down her jaw. "I haven't taken very good care you. I'm sorry."

She wanted to protest — he'd taken excellent care of her. Her body had never felt so alive as when he or Denith was touching her, but she couldn't find the words to tell him.

Rainek placed a quick kiss on her mouth and then stood. Tiana couldn't do anything but lie there, dazed and amazed, her mind and body worn out from the past three days. Had it only been three days? She couldn't remember her life before Rainek.

She watched as he relit the torch, then carried water and more fruit to her and knelt down beside her. His naked skin was a mix of gold and shadow in the pale torchlight and Tiana felt her mouth water. He was beautiful. Even in her tired state she felt her sex clench at the sweet sight. *Delicious.* She licked her lips, wanting him more than she wanted fruit. The memory of sucking his cock back at the Keep seeped into her consciousness. She opened her mouth as he offered her some fruit, drawing it inside, imagining it was his shaft. He gave her water and she dutifully drank but she couldn't look away. She watched, fascinated by the soft play of firelight across his skin.

"Now, none of that," he remonstrated, though there was laughter in his voice. "You're exhausted."

"You're beautiful," she replied, startled by the deep, husky tone that came from her throat.

The light in his eyes flared, turning hot black for a moment then he shook his head.

"Later. After you've rested."

Disappointment curled her mouth downward and Rainek felt his cock rise.

Damn, she looked ready to pout. Denith rumbled inside his head, sending his approval for the direction of Tiana's thoughts. Rainek crushed the dragon's suggestions. It was *his* fault they were in this mess—with Tiana so exhausted she could barely keep her eyes open.

He slipped another piece of fruit between her lips and silently cursed himself and Denith for their use of her. But he couldn't have stopped the dragon. The memories of last night— with men threatening his mate—had returned along with the sweet sensuality of watching her bathe and Denith had grown desperate. The only way to sooth an upset dragon was to allow him access to his mate's cunt. Because it was only danger to a mate that put the dragon in that mood.

Rainek couldn't remember how many times she'd come under Denith's tongue but she'd been screaming for mercy by the time the dragon had finished with her.

But there was something different in her eyes now. Lust was there but something else. A deeper emotion maybe? Rainek scoffed at his own thoughts. His desperate heart was trying to see love in her eyes, searching for it when they'd known each other for three days, two of which had been spent in this cave. He knew she liked to fuck him—and he was damned glad of that—but soon, his human side would crave more.

He was already in love with her. Partially because of the dragon's intuitive nature, but also because of her gentle laughter and quick smile. She'd accepted him, not only by taking him into her body but by not turning away when she saw that he and Denith were the same creature. Instead of fleeing, she'd healed him. Them.

He never would have imagined himself in love with someone like her. He'd always expected someone tougher, more of a warrior woman. Tiana was more home and hearth and he found he craved that. He craved her.

He looked into her eyes and saw a reflection of his own desires. He dismissed it. She couldn't want more. She had to be drained. Her eyes skimmed down his body, and damn, he wished she would stop licking her lips like she wanted to taste him. His cock was already hard, the memory of Denith's tongue in her pussy lingering at the forefront of his mind. It had been too long since he'd been inside her.

Rainek clamped down on the sensation and continued to feed her. He needed to take care of her. She was his mate, his woman. Unfortunately, even watching her eat was a sensual experience and it was all he could do not to lean over and lick the fruit juice from her mouth.

When she'd had her fill, Rainek pushed the remaining fruit to the side and pulled the blanket up over her shoulders. Stroking his hand down her hair, he started to turn away. He had to get away. The desire to mount her again was surging through his body and she was doing nothing to diminish that urge.

The flicker of silver against her pale skin drew his eyes. The amulet. That she could wear it at all was amazing. None but the three siblings had ever been able to tolerate it for long. Seeing it against her creamy breasts, he knew he wanted it on her skin always.

He reached out and traced his finger along the silver dragon.

Mine. Denith's voice echoed off the stone walls.

Guilt rushed into her cheeks and Tiana grabbed at the chain.

"I wasn't trying to keep it…"

Rainek covered her hands with his. "No. He wasn't talking about the amulet. He was talking about you."

Chapter Eight

Tiana felt her cheeks heat at Rainek's soft statement. She had faint memories of Denith saying the same thing...and her agreeing to it.

But what did it mean? It seemed like the dragon had claimed her — but what about the man? And how long would the dragon's possession last? Tiana didn't know if she could ask those questions. Not sure she wanted the answers. She didn't have long with him and she didn't want to spend that short time worrying about the future.

Ignoring the concerns that tried to push to the surface, she let the sensuality of the past three days lead her. She pressed up on her toes and kissed him. It was the first time since that night in the chamber that she'd come to him. The power was delicious. She wrapped her arms around his neck and teased her tongue into his mouth. He instantly joined her in the caress. The hard muscles of his chest excited the peaks of her breasts and it was all she could do to hold back a groan.

He cupped her backside and pulled her up and forward, until his erection was nestled between her thighs reigniting the desire eased by the dragon's possession. Her leg rode up his until she curled around his hip. Rainek tore his mouth away and grabbed a deep breath.

"We can't. You have to be exhausted."

"More," she whispered against his neck, opening her mouth and nipping his taut skin.

Rainek dropped his head to the side and groaned. "See, this is what happens when you introduce a virgin to really hot sex. They don't want to stop."

Tiana leaned away and stared up. His teasing grin made her wince. Virginity was a prize amongst so many kingdoms but she couldn't deceive him.

"Uh, Rainek...I wasn't a virgin when we came together."

He flinched as if startled by her statement and she mentally sighed. What was it with men? They all wanted virgins—experienced virgins, that is. He chuckled.

"Uh, no, honey, I know that. I meant me."

She dropped her leg and stepped back, ignoring for a moment that her pussy was wet and aching. "What?"

He shrugged. "I was a virgin."

"When?" She didn't believe it. She couldn't believe it. A man like this? He would have women after him from the time he crawled from the cradle. He had to be lying. No man, and certainly no man who looked like him and fucked like him, would have waited thirty summers before having sex.

But the hint of red in his cheeks made her curious.

"That time in the chamber, when I had you up against the wall—"

Tiana felt his words like a potent memory in her pussy.

"It was the first time I'd ever had sex."

"That's impossible." He'd been too good. He'd lasted too long.

He laughed again, but there was little humor in the sound. "No, that's what it's like being half-dragon. The dragon gets control of that part of your body. Ask my brother—he's still waiting."

"I don't believe it." She folded her arms under her chest—which served to push her breasts high and forward. Rainek's eyes dipped down and then farther down, lingering for a moment on the apex of her thighs.

Irritation flickered inside her chest. There was no way he was inexperienced. But why would he lie about something like that?

Needing his attention back to their very confusing conversation, Tiana dropped one hand and covered her pussy. The movement drew his focus back up.

"Sorry," he said with no sincerity. She ignored it.

"Now, tell me the truth," she insisted.

"I am. Denith wasn't going to let me have sex until he'd found the right woman." He walked back to the blankets and threw himself to ground, sitting on the stone floor. Despite the casual pattern of his words, his cock was still thick and hard.

"My mother studied dragons for years before she met my father. He'd suffered a dragon bite and between the two of them, they discovered that a dragon's mission in life is to find its mate and make more little dragons. That's how the whole sacrificing virgins thing started. If the dragon could find a woman he liked, he was much more content, and much less likely to steal your cattle and burn your farmland.

"But with us—my brother and I—since the dragon has been around since the beginning, we were born searching for the dragon's mate. Until he found her, no sex." He smiled and the wicked sensuality that flowed through his eyes renewed the need in the pit of her stomach. "Until now."

"Why now?" *Why me?*

"Denith chose you as his mate. We've been searching for as long as I can remember to find the one woman who could satisfy me and the dragon."

A strange sensation, not far from fear, filled her chest.

"Mate? Dragons pick a mate?" It was too difficult to comprehend. Everything she'd ever heard was that dragons stole—and fucked—women indiscriminately. And she thought she'd been one of those. To have been chosen by the dragon...she wasn't sure how she felt about that. Normal human males had rarely looked twice at her but somehow the dragon found her acceptable. "So what does that mean now that he's picked a mate?"

The lazy smile Rainek gave her made her insides melt. He leaned back on one elbow as if presenting himself for her inspection. "You'll be loved, well and often by Denith, and me, of course."

"How long?"

Rainek's expression turned from lazy to confused.

"How long what? How long are you mated?"

She nodded. She didn't think it was that strange of a question. If the dragon was going to keep her, she wanted a time frame.

"Forever. There will be no other women. Only you. I have no desire for any other. Nor does Denith."

Tiana couldn't catch her breath. She'd never imagined hearing those words...not spoken to her. Even the joinings sanctioned by the queen were open. No one expected a woman to have only one lover in her life. It was generally held that women weren't made to be monogamous. There were so many men around eager to serve.

But Tiana knew she would never want another lover. She'd held Rainek inside her body and there would never be another like him.

"I don't understand." The words slipped out.

"You'll be the only woman I will make love to."

"But Merena..."

Rainek shook his head. "Only you. Forever."

The concept was completely foreign. A man who wanted nothing but to be with her. Her. It was something to think about.

Of course, he wasn't fully a man, but somehow when he stared at her with such intensity, that fact didn't matter.

He held out his hand, palm up. "Come, I need more of you."

She didn't know what drew her but she couldn't seem to resist. Thoughts clattered through her head—mates and dragons, Rainek and sex. When he called, her body reacted. She walked to his side and knelt down.

Her hands burned, her power inflamed by the steady stream of pleasure the dragon had given her. She knew better than to touch him. She ignored his outstretched hand and sank down, lying beside him on her side.

Rainek turned so they faced each other. He reached up and cupped her chin with his palm. The action was so gentle, so tender, Tiana felt the foreign sensation of tears in her eyes.

Never before had a lover treated her as if she was a delicate creature. Rainek let his hand skim down her body, pausing to cup her breasts and tease her nipples. She watched the half-smile curve his mouth as the peaks poked out, seeking more of his attention.

"Beautiful," he said, almost to himself.

Tiana felt the power of that word in her heart. She felt beautiful in a way she never had before. He continued the slow wandering caresses, sliding down her waist, over her hip and along her leg. He didn't stop, as she had expected him to, at her pussy — instead he wound one long finger across her thigh, creating a path of heat across her skin as he decorated her with invisible lines of fire.

With a gentle nudge on her hip, he rolled her to her back. Tiana spread her legs, anticipating the request. Again he smiled but still skirted her sensitive core. The slow exploration expanded, reaching farther, as if he simply wanted to learn her, to touch her. Give her pleasure. He returned, following a new trail up her stomach and to the valley between her breasts.

He leaned over and placed a soft kiss on her mouth, but when she opened her lips to accept more, he pulled back.

"Denith would like to have you."

Despite what she'd seen, she didn't quite understand how he and the dragon could inhabit the same body. Was the dragon listening to them now?

"I'll still be here," he assured her, "but he would like to feel you as only I can. Will you allow it?"

So much had happened in the past three days that she found herself agreeing.

"Will I recognize a difference?" she asked.

"My eyes. When Denith is present, my eyes change."

As the words left his mouth, it happened. The fiery amber disappeared and all that was left was black. The glowing black of the dragon's eyes. He leaned forward and covered her mouth with his. The kiss was deep and desperate as if he needed to gather all the sensations at once. When she was gasping for air but didn't care because his mouth felt so good, he pulled back and looked down at her.

"Denith?"

He slowly nodded. "Have you." The voice was Rainek's but there was a subtle difference as if he wasn't sure of the inflection to give his words. "Come inside you, my mate. Mine."

She allowed her legs to fall open. He stared down, looking at her cunt as if it was the most beautiful object he'd ever seen. Tiana shifted—enjoying the desperate hunger in his eyes. He didn't move.

She sat up and hooked her hand around Rainek's neck, drawing him to her. She placed her mouth against his, lightly touching. He waited, allowing her to do what she would. It struck her that these sensations were new to the dragon.

They lay beside each other, just kissing and stroking. Denith seemed fascinated by the skin just above her knee. She'd never thought of it as a particularly arousing place but when he leaned down and brushed the area with a kiss, she changed her mind. His tongue swept across the same spot.

"Delicious." The sentiment was all Denith. She shivered as he laved his tongue over her skin, mixing the caresses with hot, open-mouthed kisses, moving steadily upward toward her pussy. Anticipation built—knowing the dragon's affection for oral loving.

Unlike Rainek, Denith didn't seem to understand teasing, he moved straight in, placing his mouth over her cunt and stroking his tongue the length of her slit. A shudder ran through his body and Tiana felt it echo in hers. Her moan seemed to encourage him and he lapped at her sex as if starving for her taste.

The eager pulses of his tongue were different from the exploring caresses of Rainek but no less exciting. She panted as he buried his face in her sex. He drove her up, fast and high, sending a glistening orgasm through her body, then licking her as she flooded his tongue with her moisture.

Staring up at the ceiling, she tried to bring herself back to this world. Denith/Rainek was still licking her but she wanted more. Wanted to feel his cock.

"Wait," she said. He ignored her so she followed the command with a tug on his hair and a squirm that succeeded in closing her thighs a little. He raised his head, a thoroughly disgruntled look on his face. "I want your cock," she said, deliberately dropping her voice to a low, hopefully sexy tone.

The dragon blinked. Amber flickered in the blackness of his eyes and she knew that Rainek hadn't fully left them.

She smiled and pulled him upward, until he was almost over her. Before he could settle on top of her, she pushed his shoulder, rolling him to his back. Black returned to his eyes and he fell back against the stone floor. She stared at his chest, loving the thick muscles and strong arms.

The wound in his side caught her attention and for a moment pulled her from her sensual fog. The site was pink and healing, though there was a scar. Obviously the dragon healed faster than the human. She placed hot kisses along his chest, allowing her breasts to skim over him. He groaned—a raw, animal sound.

He watched her with greedy eyes as if he didn't want to miss anything. She brushed her damp curls away from her head and smiled.

Power again surged through her. She had two strong dangerous creatures waiting for her, at her mercy.

"I want to ride you," she said, loving his eyes on her.

She pushed herself up and slowly swung her leg over him until she straddled his hips. His hot gaze ignited another burst of desire inside her. She was finally going to mount him. This was how she had been taught to fuck a man and the thought of having him below her, ready to pleasure her, sent a new shiver into her sex. His cock was hard and arched up, pressing almost to his stomach. She wanted to wrap her hands around it, stroke its beautiful length. She'd forgotten the danger of her touch for a moment but the truth returned. To touch him would turn his passion into pain. Instead, she slid down, until her knees surrounded his thighs and his cock was presented before her.

"Would you like to feel my mouth on you?" She let her voice be a whisper as she bent down. She didn't wait for his answer as she placed the flat of her tongue on the underside and ran up the full hot length. Carefully, she used one finger to lift the end and quickly sucked the thick head into her mouth, tickling the underside with her tongue. Memories of his heavy groans in the training chamber returned. She knew what to do to give him pleasure and she used it on him now, sucking him, licking him. Teasing him but never allowing him satisfaction. She lost herself in the feel of having him in her mouth, in her power.

The heavy groans that poured from his lips gave her courage and she sank deeper, swallowing as much of him as she could. Unconsciously, she rolled her hips, imagining the thick ride of his shaft inside her. She ached to feel him inside her but was unwilling to release her prize—he felt too delicious in her mouth.

"Mine?" The question made her pull back and sit up taller.

The light in his eyes was no longer black, no longer amber—but red.

"Mine, I think," she said with a final swipe of her tongue. Sighing with regret, she lifted her hips and crawled up, her breasts hanging close to his mouth and her pussy once again over his shaft. The bright moisture left behind from her sucking glittered in the pale light, highlighting the deep purple shade of his cock.

"Put it inside me," she commanded, raising herself up on her knees and placing her hands harmlessly on her thighs. His eyes flickered and flared with excitement as he reached down and collected his cock. He directed the tip to her wet opening. "Slowly," she ordered, then swirled her hips, teasing the tip of his cock on her clit. His breath hissed through his tightly clenched teeth and Tiana knew she couldn't leave him in pain much longer.

Knowing this would be Denith's first time to fuck her, she watched him. She'd ridden men before but this was different. Her previous lovers had looked at her with casual lust or hunger. But Denith's stare was like an arrow in her chest — deep and hard — and permanent. It was beyond lust or mere desire.

She opened her legs wider and held still as Rainek directed his cock into her opening. His free hand wrapped around her hip as if to hold her in place, then he pulled her downward at the same time arching his hips up. The first few inches of his shaft slid into her pussy. It was amazing — the strange mix of the new and the familiar. She knew how he fit inside her but, as she rode him, he felt larger than before. And while she should have been in control, his hot stare warned her he was at his limit. She allowed him to guide her down, settling more of him inside her. He didn't rush but he didn't stop either. The color of his eyes switched from black to amber and back.

Both creatures were struggling for control.

A surge of feminine power shot into her.

She laughed and pushed downward, cramming the last two inches inside her. Rainek was having just as much difficulty finding his breath as she was. Now that he was inside her, she felt no reason to rush. She slowly circled her hips, rubbing her clit against the base of his cock.

Rainek tensed and grabbed her hips. She froze and stared down at him.

"Mine," she announced. This would be her fuck and her cock.

Rainek pulled his hands away and let them fall onto the blanket.

Careful not to touch him, she leaned forward and placed her hands on the stone floor next to his head. She raised her hips and began to pump—short and shallow, just enough to rub that spot deep inside her passage. At first she moved this way because she knew it would drive him crazy not to feel a full thrust but then she lost herself in the motion. She had to have more. The steady pressure inside her cunt built until her hips pounded his.

Tiana pushed herself back, sitting up and driving him fully inside her. And again she stopped. Rainek raised his eyes to hers in panic. She allowed herself the hint of a smile just to torment him.

"You feel so good inside me," she whispered, her voice bouncing along the stone walls. She placed her hands on her thighs feeling like the legendary warriors of her land, her supplicant beneath her, ready to serve for her pleasure. Rainek, and Denith, had given her this strength. His eyes shut as she worked him hard inside her.

"Watch me." His eyelids popped open and his gaze met hers. "I want to see who I'm fucking. See who is coming inside me." She flicked a finger down his stomach. "Do you want to come inside me?"

"Tiana—" The deep way he growled her name made it a command.

But she was in charge for now. And she was enjoying this too much. It was amazing that her body was still able to function, was still willing to accept him inside but she was slick as she continued to thrust herself down, impaling herself on his cock.

"Do you? Do you want to come inside my pussy?"

"Yes." His groan was sweet and she gave him a little more. Her breasts bounced as she moved on him. Knowing he watched, she reached up and cupped the mounds with her hands.

His fingers clutched the blankets as if to keep himself from grabbing her. She leaned forward, needing her arms to give her the leverage to truly ride him. Their breath intermingled as they each strained for their release.

His hips punched up as she pounded down. It felt so good to have him inside her. She needed her climax but she wanted his, wanted his surrender. She fought the pleasure, holding it back as she pumped faster.

"By the Goddesses, come," she commanded, though it sounded almost like a plea.

"I will when you will," he answered almost daring her.

Shocked at his rough, teasing tone, she met his gaze and nodded. They moved together, once, twice and on the third stroke, she pressed down, forcing her clit to ride the penetration. He shouted as he exploded inside her. Her scream joined his cry as she accepted his cum and felt her own release shatter inside her sex.

Too exhausted to hold herself upright, she collapsed down, falling onto his chest. Time passed in a blur as she struggled to regain her breath. Rainek stroked his hands down her back, cupping her backside and lingering there. He pressed her hard against him, keeping his cock in her pussy, and rolled, pushing her back to the ground.

She blinked up at him though she wasn't surprised. He didn't need much time to recover.

"We want more of you," he whispered seconds before he bent down and covered her mouth in a deep, enticing kiss. Tiana could do nothing but respond—giving him what they all wanted.

* * * * *

Tiana closed her eyes and let her head fall back. Rainek was on top of her, still inside her, her legs still curled around his waist. She never wanted to let him go. He buried his face along the curve of her neck and sighed. For the moment she didn't know if it was Rainek or Denith and it didn't matter.

Her body obviously didn't care. They'd each taken her, loved her with unique styles—Rainek teasing and tempting until she was screaming for a release, and Denith with the hard pounding fuck of a creature who indulged his senses to the fullest. Sometimes, in the middle, one would take over from the other.

The power struggle she watched in his eyes was fascinating and seductive. Two powerful creatures wanted to fuck her. And she'd let them. Wanted them. And her body wouldn't let her forget it. Her throat was tender from the screams and shouts inspired by her climaxes. Her hands burned with blue flame; waves of heat radiating from her palms. She stretched up and placed her hands against the cave wall. The rock crackled beneath her palms. The release did little to ease her pain but at least she wouldn't set fire to the blanket if she accidentally touched it.

After a few moments, she relaxed and let her hands fall, palm up, on the stone beside her head. She dropped into a light doze, exhaustion finally winning.

Sounds outside the cave came as whispers, so soft that Tiana didn't recognize them until it was too late. Within seconds the room was full of people, warriors of Merena's guard formed a half circle around them, arrows notched and drawn back. Rainek rolled off her—the blackness in his eyes alerting her that Denith was present and ready to protect her. The dragon's cry ripped through the cave and shattered against the walls. Two of the warriors flinched, covering their ears as he screamed.

The noise covered the twang of a bow and the thunk of an arrow piercing Rainek's thigh. He stared down at the foreign object. Tiana sat up, throwing herself in front of Rainek.

"Leave him alone."

"Oh, we will." The line separated and Merena strolled in. How out of place she looked dressed in her long pale gown with her slippered feet on the stone floor. "He won't give us any more trouble."

Tiana spun around. Rainek was on his knees staring at the arrow in his leg. He blinked and swayed and his eyes began to cloud.

"What did you do to him?" Tiana demanded.

"I merely ensured that there won't be a problem getting him back to the Keep."

Rainek's eyes burned amber and then rolled upward. He tipped over, falling hard to the floor. His eyes closed and within seconds he was limp on the ground.

Merena sighed. "That probably bruised him. Well, it looks like I'll have more wounds to soothe on his scrumptious body."

Tiana glared up at the princess. "Stay away from him." She heard the soft hum of bowstrings tightening and knew the arrows were now directed at her.

"Don't be foolish. The poison on the arrow tips will only incapacitate him for a little while. But you're only human. It will kill you."

"You know?" Tiana whispered.

Merena laughed and the sound felt like nails in Tiana's flesh. "Why do you think I captured him?" Merena leaned forward until only Tiana could hear her words. "Imagine the strength of my bloodline when my child inherits my powers and his dragon strength."

And it all made sense. This was why Rainek had been captured, why Merena was willing to take the risk of kidnapping a prince from another realm. And why she knew the queen would approve her choice. Merena hadn't just gone for a wellborn sex toy—she was looking for a royal consort. And a dragon to boost the power of her bloodline.

As soon as she understood Merena's plan, Tiana remembered the political turmoil months ago when the queen had offered one of her daughters to Kei for marriage to one of his sons. The daughters of Queen Leika were prized around the world but King Kei refused the agreement, saying his sons would choose their own brides. Rainek had been on his way to meet each of Leika's daughters when Merena had grabbed him. She obviously wasn't taking any chances that Rainek might refuse her.

But the only way the queen could compel a marriage was if there was a child. "You were trying to steal his seed."

Merena laughed and stepped back. "He's probably scattered it to the four winds already. I'll just be taking a little of it and starting a dynasty. Surely that's worth a few fucks." She smiled and Tiana felt a chill go down her spine. "I'll make sure he enjoys it." She nodded toward Tiana. "It appears from the marks on your body, that he's quite a commanding lover. That should be interesting. Once we're wed I might actually let him ride me instead of the other way around."

Hearing Merena's plans to fuck Rainek and fill herself with his seed made Tiana's stomach turn.

Merena looked over her shoulder to Sienna, captain of the guard. "Take her into custody."

Sienna hesitated. "What is the charge?"

"Treason." Merena stared smugly at Tiana. "She kidnapped my consort and seduced him."

Sienna nodded and ordered two of the guards to take hold of Tiana. The captain walked up as they pulled Tiana's arms behind her back. "Don't fight us. We don't want to hurt you," she whispered.

Tiana nodded. They were merely doing their job. She stood calmly and let them bind her wrists.

"Is there something we can give her for cover when we enter the Keep grounds?" Sienna asked.

Merena smirked. "No. She's a slut who seduced a royal consort. The world should know what her crimes are."

Tiana blushed but kept her mouth shut. A pallet was brought in and four male slaves, dressed only in loincloths and neck chains, placed Rainek on it and carried him away. Tiana couldn't stop herself from watching as they walked out of the cave.

Merena watched her. "Don't worry. Once I have his heir inside me, he can fuck whoever he wants. He might even want to come back to you. Our scouts got a sample of your enthusiasm as they waited for the troop to arrive. You're quite the energetic lover if the cries they described are any indication. Maybe you can work off your sentence as a thrall in the slave house. But after they've all had you, I doubt Rainek would want you back."

Her upper lip curled as she stared at Tiana's naked body. Then her eyes landed on the medallion around her neck. "What's that? That's not something you owned."

Tiana tried to step back but the guards were behind her. Merena reached out and pulled the heavy chain up and over Tiana's head. "It's lovely. Looks like something a bride should wear, don't you think?" She draped the chain around her neck and let the amulet fall onto her breasts. "Ow." She pulled it away. Red marked her skin where the medallion had touched. Suspicion laced her eyes when she finally looked up at Tiana. Tiana glanced down at her own breasts. The amulet hadn't left any marks on her skin. "Well, it doesn't go with my gown." She removed the chain and held it in her hand. "Bring her," she commanded, then spun around and floated out of the cavern.

With the prodding of the guards, Tiana followed moments later. It had all happened so suddenly. She'd gone from sex goddess to prisoner. A touch of regret crept into her heart as she left the cave. Not for what she'd done but because her time with Rainek was over.

Merena's carriage glittered gold against the blue sky. The wicked princess held the door open until Tiana exited the cave, long enough for her to see inside, to see Rainek slouched on the seat, his body propped against the far wall. Merena reached out and ran one long fingertip down his cock then dragged her finger up to her own mouth.

Without another word, she slammed the door shut and commanded the driver onward. Mud flung from the carriage wheels splattered across Tiana's ankles.

"Let's go," Sienna said, nudging Tiana forward. "We've got a long walk ahead of us." Merena would arrive in a tenth of the time it would take them to walk the same distance to the Keep. By then she'd have Rainek aroused and probably coming inside her.

Tiana felt her heart plummet into her stomach and started walking, dragging her feet with each step. Rainek had vowed that he would not accept Merena—that he wouldn't fuck her. He'd claimed Tiana was his mate and that he would have no other.

Her heart clung to that hope even when she wanted to banish it from her mind. She didn't want to think about him or hold onto a useless dream. Merena would drug him. Again. And he'd be unable to resist her.

Even knowing the little she did about Rainek, she knew he was honorable. If Merena became pregnant with his child, he would marry her. No matter what the dragon said.

Sienna fell into step. Tiana glanced at the guard captain. They were friends but treason was a charge that made friends back away. No one wanted to be associated with an enemy of the Matriarchy. Tiana had broken one of the most fundamental rules of their world—you kept your hands off another woman's man. Not that he'd ever belonged to Merena, Tiana mentally defended. If Rainek was telling the truth, he'd been a virgin when they'd gotten together.

But he'd learned quickly, she thought with a self-indulgent smile. Sienna's eyes tightened in confusion. One wasn't supposed to smile as one was being led off to prison. *Add another sin to my crimes.*

"You know, Tiana, I never imagined you'd be tempted into treason. What made you think you could get away with seducing a consort?"

Tiana stared at her friend in stunned amazement. "Sienna, you don't seriously believe that I could kidnap that man. He ripped the chains out of the chamber wall. What could I have done to force him to come with me?"

"I don't think you kidnapped him," Sienna acknowledged. "You might not have gone with him willingly, even, but I was on the scouting crew. I heard you two inside that cave." Half her mouth curled upward. "Those weren't screams of protest."

"No," Tiana sighed. There was no regret. It had been three days of pure pleasure.

Sienna glanced around as if to assure they were alone then dropped her voice. "Just between you and me, were you faking it? Or was he that good?"

Tiana grinned and didn't bother to hide the smugness in her voice. "He's that good."

Chapter Nine

"Prince Rainek?" The softly seductive voice traveled as a whisper across his skin, slipping into his head. "Wake up, darling. You're home."

His eyes fluttered open adapting quickly to pale golden light that illuminated the elegant bedchamber. A strange fog covered his mind making everything from his thoughts to his vision hazy.

Where was he? Who was he? *Rainek.* She'd called him Rainek. Prince Rainek. The name sounded familiar.

He turned his head and stared at the woman next to him. She looked vaguely familiar as well but his mind couldn't capture the appropriate memory. She lay in bed beside him, the blankets covering her body up to her bare shoulders. Her beautiful black hair shining in the candlelight.

Black hair hung just to her chin, smooth and straight and with a soft swing to it as she strolled toward him.

The memory brushed through him. He knew this woman. He just didn't know why? Or why she was in bed with him?

"Darling, are you all right?" Concern filled her voice.

"I believe so," he said, not wanting to confess he remembered none of this...not even the woman who called him "darling".

She stroked her hand over his bare chest. The cool brush of her fingers felt foreign — as if her hands should be warm.

"I know you've had a terrible ordeal, but you're safe now. Back where you belong."

And where is that? He tried to push through the fog but it seemed to swell until the room began to spin around him.

"What happened?" he asked, closing his eyes, trying to slow circular motion.

"You were kidnapped by one of our maids, but don't worry...you're back where you belong." She'd said that before. "Here with me." Her hand slipped farther down, until long fingers wrapped around his cock and began to stroke it. "I've missed you. Missed having you inside me."

No. Not mine.

The strange voice in his head screamed but the sound came to him vague and distant.

He opened his eyes—grateful that the room had stopped its twirl—as the covers were tossed back. The woman pushed herself up in a slow, seductive movement until she knelt beside him. She kept caressing his flaccid cock but instead of the lust he'd heard in her voice...he saw determination in her eyes. She blinked and it went away.

"Don't you want me, darling?" She pulled her hand away from his groin and placed it on her own skin. Using both hands, she cupped her high tight breasts. She was beautiful, Rainek acknowledged but still, there was no reaction from his recalcitrant shaft. "I've missed you so much."

Feeling like a heel for not being able to perform for the lady, he grimaced and sighed. "I think I'm still tired."

She dropped her shoulders and a hard glint filled her gaze.

Suddenly, she seemed much more familiar, but he couldn't figure out why.

Then, like before, in a blink it was gone.

"I understand." Her voice was soothing and with a singsong air that lulled him. "Let's give you something that will make you feel better." She handed him a glass filled with a bright green liquid. "Take your medicine." He downed the drink in one gulp. The glass was taken from his hand and another instantly placed there. This time it was clear. "Just a little something to help you sleep," she encouraged.

Rainek didn't understand that. He didn't need anything to help him sleep. He was exhausted. And confused. But he drank it. The liquid burned as it flowed down his throat.

"Sleep now and I'll return in a little while after you've rested." She stood up and pulled a long silk robe around her naked body. Again he was struck by the elegant beauty of her...and his own lack of desire. "It's so good to have you back where you belong."

Where you belong.

I belong here. With her.

No, somehow, that didn't sound right.

* * * * *

Tiana stared at the bars that made up her temporary home. The Matriarchy had few prisons but what they lacked in quantity, they made up for in quality. It had been years since anyone had been placed in these cells and the dust, grime and mouse droppings were evidence of that. It had taken her a solid day to clean the cell so she didn't sneeze every time she'd moved.

Thankfully, the guards had given her water and rags. The activity had kept her busy as well. Unfortunately, it was fairly mindless work and that gave her time to think about what Merena was doing to Rainek. And what Rainek was doing to Merena.

He promised there would be only you.

That damned hopeful voice kept nagging her whenever she tried to drive him from her thoughts. It just made it worse. It would be so much easier if she could just accept that Rainek would end up marrying Merena and producing two perfect little dragon babies. She knew Merena well enough to know she'd never risk her figure by having more than two children.

Tiana stood up and gathered her bucket and rags. There was nothing else to do. She began polishing the bars, washing away years of grime.

"Isn't this sweet? Hoping to get assigned as a maid when you're released?" Merena stepped into the light. "It will never happen. No one will want you. You can't be trusted, even around males bound to another woman."

Tiana didn't flinch and she didn't stop her cleaning. "Yes, a treason charge, even a false one, tends to hang on one," she said casually.

"False?" Merena folded her arms across her chest and glared. "Do you deny that you were fucking him? After you knew he belonged to me."

It didn't matter that she was imprisoned or even that Merena was going to take what she needed whether Rainek wanted to give it or not, Tiana dropped her rag and crossed her arms in a position mirroring Merena's.

"He never belonged to you. And he never will." It was false confidence speaking, inspired by that damned hope that wouldn't leave her chest.

"Oh, he will. In fact, he does. He hasn't even asked about you." She lowered her hands and wandered in front of the cell door. "It's been three days and ask anyone...we've spent them all together, inside his bedchamber."

The hope that had flickered insistently in her chest for three days wavered.

"I want to see Rainek." Tiana couldn't believe the demand had come from her mouth but she also couldn't believe that he would have left her here. Even if he didn't want her any more, he wouldn't have allowed her to sit in a cell. Not when he shared the responsibility for what had put her there. She knew enough of him and Denith to know one of them would come for her.

"I'm not sure that's possible. Prince Rainek has been quite busy over the past few days." She smoothed her hands down her hips to give Tiana an idea of what Rainek had been doing.

"I want to see him." She needed to hear it from his mouth.

Merena stared at her for a long time then sighed. "Fine. The guards will escort you to get cleaned up and then they'll bring you to his chamber. Will that satisfy you?"

The muscles in her shoulders tightened. Merena was too confident. She would never allow Tiana to speak with Rainek unless she was sure of the outcome. Still, Tiana couldn't resist it. Why she was torturing herself like this, she didn't know, but she had to see him. Had to see for herself that he'd accepted Merena. He'd sounded so sincere when he'd sworn there would be no woman except for Tiana. *A dragon's mate.*

It was all his fault. She'd never considered binding herself to one man but the way he'd spoken, promising himself to her...she'd fallen for the dream and now she was clinging to it as her only lifeline.

"You're not being released, you understand. You are guilty of treason, after all." She skimmed her eyes down Tiana's naked body. Tiana didn't flinch. After three days in the cell and three days with Rainek, she'd gotten quite used to being unclothed. "You'll come to his chamber and see for yourself."

Merena curved her lips into a mockery of a smile then turned and walked away.

The guard stepped forward and indicated that Tiana was to leave.

She hurried to her rooms, thankful that everything was left as it was. She wanted to race through her bath and get to Rainek but the last time she'd fully bathed was the river outside the cavern three days ago. It took a while to wash and comb the tangles from her hair and three rinses before she felt clean. Finally, she pulled on her prettiest gown—Rainek hadn't seen her dressed in anything but rough wool and nothing—and opened her door.

Sienna, the guard captain, waited for her. The grim look on her face didn't bode well.

"Are you sure you want to do this?" she asked. "They've been together constantly and every report says he's content where he is."

"I need to see him," Tiana said with conviction.

Sienna shrugged and led her down the hall. Tiana knew the way, of course, but followed behind Sienna. They passed a group of women in the hall. The women, once friendly to Tiana, frowned when they saw her. As they walked away, furious whispers echoed back to Tiana and her guard.

In their eyes, she'd committed the ultimate sin—seducing another woman's chosen lover.

She raised her chin and kept walking. She didn't care what they thought. Her thoughts were completely focused on seeing Rainek—finding out if he'd kept his promises.

They reached the chamber door. Sienna paused and stared with silent question at Tiana. Tiana nodded and Sienna knocked.

"Come in," Merena's sultry voice called.

The door swung open and Tiana felt her heart disappear.

Rainek lay naked on the bed, with an equally naked Merena beside him. His beautiful muscular body was flat on the mattress with Merena leaning over him. His lips were wrapped around her nipple, sucking gently.

"Oh, I'm sorry. You were so filthy, I thought you'd take longer." Merena smoothed her hand down Rainek's hair, then leaned back, giving Tiana a full view of him. Silver glittered around Merena's neck and Tiana realized she was wearing the amulet.

Tiana crushed the pain and fury and did her best to ignore the princess.

"Rainek?" She wanted to go to him and rip him out of the other woman's arms but she was frozen in place.

Rainek turned his head at Tiana's cry. He looked across the room and stared directly at her.

"Yes?" he asked curiously.

The question knocked what little breath she had in her chest free. He watched her, tilting his head as if confused at why she was standing in his bedchamber.

"You bastard." She whispered the curse and spun away, stalking out of the room. All his broken promises crushed the flicker of hope that had burned insistently in her chest.

* * * * *

"Who was that?" Rainek asked as the door slammed shut behind the cute little blonde.

Mine.

He ignored the voice inside his head that was becoming more and more persistent with each passing day.

"Oh, she's just a maid. No one important." Merena smiled and stroked her fingers along his forehead.

"She seemed angry with me." He felt his words blurring a bit as he spoke. According to Merena, it was a result of his kidnapping and would fade eventually but he wanted it to go now...wanted to be able to think clearly. Something seemed wrong but he couldn't work past the fog.

"She's not well, mentally. We try to keep her away from guests."

"But I'm not really a guest, am I?"

Merena's eyes grew wide. "Oh, no, of course. But somehow she's become very focused on you. She tends to bother you a lot." She grabbed her lower lip with her teeth, looking adorable and innocent. "Now, enough about her. We were in the middle of something."

He looked down at her pert, tight breasts. He'd been sucking on her nipples when they'd been interrupted, but honestly, he couldn't gather much enthusiasm for the task. It didn't seem familiar, or even that interesting.

And every time he'd tried to bolster his enthusiasm, it was as if something inside him crushed it. It felt like he was fighting his own nature to make his cock hard to fuck the woman he was supposed to marry.

Ignoring his failure to continue, Merena wrapped her hand around his cock and began to stroke. Thankfully, she seemed patient that he couldn't perform.

"Maybe something happened while I was injured that's making it..." He nodded toward his groin. "You know."

Merena nodded and again her eyes turned a flinty green. "Don't worry," she said, though her voice had lost that soothing, seductive tone. It almost sounded like she was talking through clenched teeth. "I'm sure we'll make this work. Just relax."

He grimaced but did as she asked. He lay back and stared up at the ceiling. He still had moments when the room spun but the fog seemed to be clearing slightly. And with it came foreign emotions. Anger, fury, fear.

"You're tensing up, darling. Let me take care of you." Her voice had returned to the husky whisper she used whenever she spoke to him. The sound was compelling and he tried to follow her advice, letting the haze overtake his mind. A picture formed in his head — of the blonde woman who'd stood at the door, eyes blazing with wounded fire.

She was naked. How did he know what she looked like naked? Her full breasts swayed with each step, making his mouth water. Tight pink nipples topped the luscious peaks. Those were the nipples he wanted to suck. He felt a flutter in his cock, a tightening, maybe even a hardening.

"Yes, that's it," Merena whispered eagerly.

The sound of her voice snapped him from his fantasy and he went limp.

He opened his eyes and started to apologize but she was already moving away.

"I think you need more of your medicine." She gave him another glass of the green liquid. "That should do the trick," she said smugly, sitting down on the bed beside him. "We'll just wait for a few minutes and try again."

He nodded his agreement though it was clear she didn't need it.

He stared at her for a moment, hoping for some memory, something about his previous life. He'd done a fair job of keeping his ailment from her but soon when he recovered and he had to interact with others, they were going to discover that he remembered nothing.

Merena pursed her lips and tapped her fingers on the mattress, obviously impatient. After long silent moments, she reached out and rubbed his cock. Her fingers were cool and he had a strange vision that the hand that should be touching him was hot.

"Anything?" she asked.

He shook his head. Merena sighed and reached for the carafe of his medicine. He silently groaned. He didn't think whatever she was giving him was helping.

She straightened and he heard a thump against her chest. Merena hissed and jerked the piece of silver away from skin. She quickly pulled the necklace off and started to place it on the table beside the bed.

"What's that?" he asked, hoping to distract her. She held up the chain.

"It's a necklace I wear. You gave it to me."

"It's a dragon." His eyes were still unfocused so he had to move closer to see it. Reaching out, he stroked the silver with his index finger.

Pain shot through his hand, up his arm and into his chest. He fell back on the bed, panting as he fought the waves of agony.

"Rainek? Are you all right? What happened?"

The soft whispery voice was gone and left behind was a mixture of panic and irritation.

"I'm fine," he answered, his mind swirling with lights and colors. This was different. The fog was gone. Each image crystal clear.

And the voice inside his head screamed.

Mine!

As if touching the medallion had burned the poison from his body or reconnected him to his soul, his life came back to him. Complete with an irritated dragon.

Are you listening to me, now? Denith demanded.

Yes.

Couldn't break through.

I know.

"What's wrong, darling?"

His stomach curled at the affectionate term. He wasn't her darling. He was Tiana's.

Oh no. Tiana.

Mine?

Maybe not any more, he thought. Not after seeing him in bed with Merena.

"Rainek?" Merena's hard tone demanded a response.

"I'm sorry. I must have strained a muscle when I reached for you. I think I should rest."

Her eyes tightened in suspicion but then she smiled.

"I'll let you sleep. Here." She handed a tumbler of the clear liquid. He held it to his nose and could smell the poison in it but knew he had no choice. His mind was clear but the rest of him was still on the influence of her potions. He swallowed the contents in one gulp and handed the glass to her. She immediately stood up and put her robe on. With a tight smile, she turned and left the room.

Rainek waited until he was sure she was gone, then grabbed the chamber pot from beneath the bed and retched up as much of the liquid as he could. When he'd lost the contents of his stomach, he sat on the side of the bed. He was weak and shaking. Whatever she'd been dosing him with had leached the strength from his body.

But his mind was clear, for the first time in three days he could think.

He had to regain his strength and find Tiana.

Denith rumbled his agreement and Rainek was never so glad to hear the dragon in his head.

* * * * *

It took another two days before he was able to walk around the room without tiring. Merena continued to dose him with the aphrodisiac and sleeping potions. The aphrodisiac had no effect and he was able to throw up most of the sleeping potions.

At noon on the third day, he stared at Merena with the vague expression he'd perfected and shrugged. "I'm sorry. I don't know what's wrong with me."

She sighed and took her hand off his crotch. "It's fine. Here." She slapped another glass of *reconi* juice into his hand. She'd lost all semblance of being sweet and loving. He drank and tried to look confused and helpless. He hated the stuff but he'd learned to counter the effects. He just never let himself think of Tiana while Merena was around. As soon as she left the room, Denith would scream and Rainek's cock got so hard he thought he would cry with the need to fuck his mate.

The potions were relatively easy to resist. The spells were harder to fight. Merena's power was strong but she tired quickly. Probably because she'd spent five days trying to convince his cock to rise. She swirled her hands over his groin. The pressure built. Rainek held his face passive but assisted Denith in his fight.

A soft knock on the door pulled Merena away. She opened the door and listened as one of the maids spoke in a whisper.

With a sharp nod, Merena shut the door. Without speaking, she pulled on her gown and finger combed her hair. Then she turned and smiled.

"My mother is here."

Rainek felt his eyes clear for a moment. "Pardon me?"

"My mother, Queen Leika is here and she'd like to meet you." Merena strolled to the bed. "She hasn't met you yet but she is willing to perform the Joining Ceremony whilst she's here."

Joining Ceremony? Over my drugged and dead body.

"I welcome the queen's arrival," he said instead.

She seemed relieved by his answer. "Good. Do you need help dressing?"

He hesitated then slowly shook his head. The illusion he'd created had to be maintained. Whatever else he'd learned, he knew Merena was dangerous. Tiana had warned him that Merena would do anything to get her desires. He never would have imagined any woman would have gone this far to marry him. It might have been flattering if he'd thought she loved him or even desired him. But he could think of no reason for her obsession. He wasn't his father's heir. She wouldn't become queen of Xicanth.

Merena smiled tightly and walked out. The door slammed behind her. Rainek let the tension flow from his body. There was no way he could join with that woman but if he could speak with the queen, he could petition for Tiana.

And then he could apologize to Tiana.

Denith rumbled his agreement. The dragon had remained remarkably contained in the past few days, not forcing Rainek to hunt down his mate and claim her.

He rolled out of bed and ran to the closet. His clothes—obviously brought along when he'd originally been kidnapped—had been neatly hung, continuing the illusion that he lived with her.

The illusion was about to shatter — in front of Queen Leika.

His brother wouldn't be happy — Bren was relying on Rainek's diplomacy after all — but he would understand. A dragon's desire for his mate took precedence over everything. Of course, after rejecting Merena, Rainek was pretty sure his family's relationship with the Matriarchy was dead.

A knock drew him to his feet. A young woman opened the door and smiled shyly. She was dressed in a plain gray gown and her hair hung limp around her face. She dropped her eyes the moment he looked at her.

"Your Highness, Her Majesty is ready for you now."

Rainek nodded and gathered himself, keeping a tight rein on Denith. He followed the maid through the halls and was led into a large chamber that obviously served as the queen's throne room. The maid waved him forward.

He walked to the front of the room. The queen sat on her throne, leaning to the side in quiet discussion with Merena. Rainek waited with the appearance of patience to be acknowledged. Finally Queen Leika and Princess Merena turned to him.

"Welcome, Prince Rainek. I send my greetings to your parents."

"They sent their greetings as well though I'm not sure they would have extended the courtesy if they'd known I'd be meeting you under these circumstances." Concern and fear flickered across Merena's face.

Queen Leika just smiled serenely. "Yes, my wicked daughter —" She looked indulgently at Merena. " —just told me about your journey here. We do have different traditions here in the Matriarchy. I'm sure you'll grow used to them, in time."

She said the last with emphasis that Rainek couldn't ignore but he just shook his head slowly.

"Now, let me assure you that your men have been released. Some of them have requested to stay here and join us. I'm sure you can work with them at a later time to get them released from their duties under your father's rule." She stood and walked forward, her elegant carriage announcing her rank even without a crown on her head. "Now, we will discuss the arrangements of your betrothal and joining to my daughter, Merena."

The dragon's roar filled his head shattering coherent thought of a moment. When he came back to himself, Queen Leika was still talking, expounding on Merena's glories. "Kings and princes from every land have desired her, begged for her hand. That she has chosen you is a great honor."

"I'm sorry, Your Majesty," he said quietly. "I am unable to marry Princess Merena. I am bound to another."

Leika looked over her shoulder. Merena stood and walked forward to stand by her mother. The resemblance between the two was amazing. The same strength and elegance—but no kindness or gentleness in their bearing.

"Yes, I heard about your escapade with Tiana. Don't worry. We have a very open view of marriage in our realm. Once Merena is with child, you may have whomever you wish in your bed, always remembering that any children born will not be allowed to rule. Now, shall we discuss a dowry?"

"Your Majesty, you don't understand. I will not marry Princess Merena."

The quiet hiss from Merena was almost lost beneath his words. She'd just realized that he was no longer under the power of her drugs and spells.

The queen's lips tightened. "You have compromised her, have you not? Have you not lain with her—has she not taken your shaft into your mouth? These are not the actions of a man who is immune to a woman."

He inwardly flinched at her words. All those things were technically true. Merena had attempted to suck his cock and she'd lain on top of him, trying to shove his soft cock into her pussy.

"Your Majesty—"

He never was able to finish that sentence. The door that he'd entered burst open and two tall men stalked in—fury hung over them like a cloud. The two women who walked behind them were smaller but no less angry.

"How dare you enter my throne room? Who are you?"

Rainek smiled. "That's my family."

Without giving the queen a chance to reply, Rainek walked forward to meet them. His father, Kei and his brother Bren led the way, ignoring the queen and focusing on Rainek.

"Are you hurt?" Kei demanded.

"No."

"You were," Bren said.

"Yes, but I'm healed."

"Where's the woman?" Kei whipped around and scanned the throne room. "I understand she was a blonde with nice..." He curled his hands in front of his chest. Lorran slapped his arm.

Rainek grinned. "Yes. They're lovely. But she's not here right now."

"Excuse me?" Queen's Leika's strident voice interrupted their conversation. "What do you mean walking into my Keep without my permission?"

Rainek almost felt sorry for her as Kei and Bren spun around to face her. Bren might be a diplomat from birth but Kei was more dragon than king right now.

"My son—" Kei folded his arms across his chest and glared down at the tall elegant queen. "Has come under some harm while in your lands."

Queen Leika raised her eyebrows but her voice was pleasant when she spoke. "No harm. I believe he's enjoyed my daughter's company. In fact he's spent five days in her bedchamber. We were just discussing the details of the Joining Ceremony when you so entered in such a timely fashion." The queen pursed her lips together and smiled up at Kei as if she knew he couldn't contradict her. Lorran obviously had no problem doing so.

"A marriage? Between Rainek and your daughter?" his mother asked.

"Yes. Surely after spending that much time in an intimate fashion, you would agree it is appropriate for them to be Joined."

"I think," Lorran announced with equal arrogance of a queen. "That we would like a chamber where we may discuss this as a family. If there is to be a Joining Ceremony, we must prepare."

Rainek started to open his mouth to protest that there was no way in any layer of the Hells that he was going to Join with Merena. No political peace was worth that misery. But before the words could leave his lips, his mother flashed him a dignified glare that made him swallow his protest.

With that silent stare she told him she wasn't happy with the situation and she would deal with him in private.

* * * * *

"So, explain to us, what in all the Dark Hells is going on?" Bren demanded quietly. "You disappear, you don't check in and then some naked woman appears in my chamber with your amulet clutched in her hands saying you've been hurt. Who was that by the way? And how did she use your amulet? And what did she mean by —"

Rainek held up his hand, stopping Bren's steady flow of questions.

"That woman is my mate, Tiana." Amid the congratulations and hugs, Rainek didn't get a chance to continue. Bren was the first to bring the conversation back.

"Then who's the dark-headed woman who claims you're marrying her? Queen Leika seems quite intent on the match."

Rainek gave them a quick version of what had happened since he'd left home. He left nothing out. Their family understood the dragon's drive for sex and would completely understand its unwillingness to perform for another woman.

His sister, Kayla, laughed softly as he described his latest predicament of every time he awoke finding Merena's mouth on his cock.

"It's not funny."

"I was just thinking how strange our family is. Every other man would be in raptures over it."

"Every other man doesn't have a rabid dragon storming around his head."

His mother placed a comforting hand on his shoulder. "I know it's hard, dear, but you've found her. Now you just need to get her."

"Preferably without causing a major incident between the two nations," Bren added.

"You mean beyond the four of you storming into the throne room?"

Kei smiled and Lorran blushed softly.

"Now, I think I can get us all out of here without having to tear down the castle walls, which I know from experience can be done." He looked at his family. "I need you all to keep the queen busy while I have a few choice words with Princess Merena."

* * * * *

Getting into the princess's chamber was no problem. She'd obviously told her servants that he was allowed in. The princess sat in front of the mirror, smoothing her already perfect hair when he stepped up behind her.

"I knew you'd come to me eventually."

He squinted his eyes at her. "Why would you think that?"

"Because I have what you want." The smug tone made him want to strangle the princess.

"Bring her to me."

Merena shook her head. "Not until you fuck me. I'm in the middle of my cycle now, I'm likely to conceive. If not, you'll continue to service me until I do. And then I'll release Tiana." She gave what he guessed was supposed to be a throaty, seductive chuckle. " — if you still want her by then." She stood up slowly, spinning to face him. Every move was calculated to show her off to best advantage. Her gown was cut low, showing a large expanse of her breasts, stopping just shy of her nipples.

Along with the beautiful image before him, he felt the pressure of magic. She was trying another spell on him.

Rainek sighed. "I know your reputation. You've seduced kings and princes from across the lands, leaving men begging for your hand but you've rejected them all. So, why do you want me?"

She gave a low chuckle. He knew was designed to be seductive. "I want to join your bloodline with mine." She sauntered forward. "Imagine it. My power and yours, combined together. The strength the most powerful witch in the kingdom and your dragon blended together. Our child will rule not only this land but yours and any other we care to control."

The feverish light of lust filled her eyes. *This* was what she hungered for — power. No man's cock could ever inspire this kind of reaction in her.

He shook his head. "It will not happen."

"Then you'll never see your precious Tiana again." Her eyes turned granite.

Denith screamed inside Rainek's brain and the sound leaked out into the room. Merena's eyes widened a bit as she stepped back.

Stay calm, Rainek told the dragon. *I won't let anything happen to Tiana.* To Merena, he folded his arms on his chest.

"You'll release Tiana, immediately. You value your reputation amongst the Seven Kingdoms. Your mother takes pride in her child who seduces and rejects kings and princes from every land. What would the world say if they knew you used potions and spells to do it? That none of your lovers chose to fuck you? You coerced them into it."

"That's not true."

Her eyes widened innocently but Rainek just grimaced. "I know from personal experience that it is. And the world will believe me. And my family." Merena looked like she was going to open her mouth to respond but Rainek stopped her. "And just in case, that threat doesn't convince you to release Tiana, unharmed, I'll provide another." He leaned forward. "You want the strength of dragon? You'll feel every bit of it as I rip the walls down around your ears. Keeping a dragon from the woman it wants is hazardous to anyone in the area."

Denith picked up the thought, silently vowing that his vengeance would be unspeakable if his delicious mate was harmed.

Merena sighed and let her shoulders fall dramatically. "Fine, I'll have her brought to the throne room."

Denith screamed his pleasure but Rainek wasn't so sure. Merena had given in a little too easily.

He nodded and spun away, keeping his senses extended behind him in case she decided to attack. His family stood in the throne room and by the looks on their faces and Queen Leika's, the conversation hadn't been entertaining. His father, mother, brother and sister all stood in one corner of the room, their arms folded and staring at the queen and her courtiers. The queen's women were dressed in fine gowns and the men all wore only loincloths, many of them with chains around their necks. The women of the Matriarchy watched Rainek's family with cautious eyes. And it was no wonder. His family looked prepared for battle.

Bren gripped his sword and stood with his legs apart. The light in his eyes flickered from green to black, warning that he was allowing Tynan to be present. Kayla wore battle leathers suitable to a man and stood beside their mother. Even Lorran, though dressed conservatively, had the look of a warrior, ready to do battle to protect her child.

Then he looked at Kei. Even though he maintained his human form, Rainek knew Nekane hovered seconds away from exploding onto the scene.

They'd been all politeness when he'd left them a short time ago.

"What happened?" Rainek asked.

"The queen's guard announced that any man brought into the queen's presence had to be dressed only in a small strip of leather. Then Queen Leika offered Mother the use of one of her pleasure slaves," Kayla explained.

"Oh."

"Yes. Things have been a little tense. Did you manage to find your mate?"

He nodded. "She's being brought here."

The tension that snapped between his family eased, even the dangerous light in his father's eyes faded to a normal color. Well, normal for a dragon.

Rainek rubbed his palms together and stared at his family.

"Listen, before Tiana gets here, I should warn you about her." He opened his hands. "She's not like us. She's...uh, different."

"As you once pointed out, we're not exactly a normal family," Bren said.

"But she's different in other ways. She's quiet. Delicate." He hesitated. "Fragile even."

His mother released a sound that was a mix of a sigh and a laugh. A sympathetic smile lit her eyes. "We're not going to be mean to your mate, Rainek."

"Well, she's probably not what you would have expected me to choose. Or even for Denith to choose."

"Rainek, we'll love her because you love her." Lorran placed her hand on his arm.

Whatever he might have said was covered by the boom as the door exploded open. Or more accurately, as the door caught fire and burned to ashes in a split second.

"That's probably her now."

Relief pushed any other concern from his head. She was unhurt. She was here. Denith shivered in ecstasy and Rainek reined in the beast.

Bren straightened and placed his hand on his sword hilt, ready to defend against attack.

Tiana stalked through the open door, stepping over the piles of burning embers. She scanned the room quickly, ignoring the queen and her ladies, stopping only when her eyes landed on Rainek.

An invisible fire raged through her body. Rainek smiled and started toward her. He made it two steps before she opened her palm and flames erupted—shooting in a line across the room, aimed directly at his head.

"You bastard!" Her shout was followed by a second burst of fire. He ducked and the tapestry on the wall behind him burst into flame.

He straightened and held out his hands, hoping to calm her—and to prove he was unarmed. "Now, Tiana, honey, let's talk about this." She was obviously still upset about seeing him in Merena's bed. He would explain—as soon as she stopped trying to set him on fire.

"Your only love. The dragon's one mate." She stalked forward and shot her hand out. The fire raced toward him. He lunged away, ducking behind a couch. The upholstery above his head began to burn. "And then I find you fucking my sister. I almost believed you."

"Let me explain—"

"I don't want to hear any more of your lies." She drew her arm back. The firefight she'd had with Denith had taught her that she should be near her limit, that her power would soon die, but she felt no weakening. Her fury gave her strength. A deep pain built in the center of her stomach.

She'd cried for two days after seeing him locked in Merena's embrace. Now, when the guards had calmly handed her a gown and released her from her cell moments ago, stating that Merena declared her free, she knew the truth. Merena had, once again, gotten what she wanted. She was pregnant with Rainek's child. There could be no other explanation.

Tiana's pain had turned to fury.

Bastard.

Her hours inside the cell had given her time to practice her newfound skill. She'd learned to contain the fire into spheres and throw them.

Rainek crawled from behind the burning couch. She sent a ball of flame into the floor inches in front of him and he jumped back. She barely noticed the others in the room, though she knew Queen Leika and her court were present. And some others—including two men—she didn't recognize. It didn't matter. Her pain needed release. She would face the consequences of her actions later. But she would have it out with Rainek before that happened.

"Now, Tiana, if you'll just—"

She drew back her arm, ready to hurl more fire in his direction, when suddenly she was bound, unable to move as two masculine arms wrapped around her chest, locking her elbows to her side.

"Your future wife is a fire witch?" the huge man holding her arms growled the question to Rainek.

The pride in Rainek's eyes pulled her out of her rage for a moment. "Yes," he responded with half a smile. He didn't seem surprised. He sounded pleased. Impressed.

"Well," Kayla said, walking to his side and slapping her hand to dampen some of the embers still burning the couch. "She's just like you described. Quiet, delicate, fragile even."

Rainek ground his teeth together and glared at his younger sister. Sarcasm, he didn't need right now.

He brushed her aside and stormed up to his mate. He was vaguely aware of other voices rumbling in the room but he ignored them.

"Now, will you let me explain?" he demanded as Tiana still struggled in Bren's hold.

"I swear I would have rather rotted in that jail than have you sleep with my sister and impregnate her."

"But, I didn't impregnate anybody." He cocked his head to the side and corrected himself. "Well, I might—"

Tiana's lips pulled back from her teeth and she growled. He glanced down at her trapped hands. Another ball of flame was forming on her palm.

"Don't burn me with that," Bren warned. "I still have need of my cock even if you're done with his."

Rainek glared at his brother to quiet him and concentrated on calming Tiana. He grabbed her wrists—to comfort her and to stop her from flaming anyone else.

"Tiana, honey, I didn't sleep with…wait, did you say sister? Merena's your sister?"

"What? It makes it worse if she's my sister?" She pulled against his grip but he didn't let her free. Careful not to hurt her, he held her still. "You still slept with her," she said. Behind her fury, he heard the pain. And maybe some tears. "You *vowed* you would be faithful. I knew you were oversexed but I didn't think you couldn't wait a few days to be between some woman's legs. A virgin. Ha!"

Rainek grimaced. Not only was Tiana truly pissed, but Kayla would never let him forget this public conversation about his sex life. But Tiana had started the conversation here. He had to finish it.

"Tiana, I didn't, haven't, *couldn't* sleep with any woman but you. You're Denith's mate."

"I *saw* you."

"No, you—" He stopped, remembering his conversation with Merena. He'd vowed to keep her practices private if she'd release Tiana, which she'd done. He would keep his end of the bargain. "Honey, you have to believe me. I wouldn't, even if I could. I would never betray you like that."

He visibly saw the anger drop from her body and she relaxed a little in Bren's arms.

The conviction on her face wavered and Rainek felt his fear ease. She was listening to him but that didn't stop her stubborn chin from lifting a little and the normal quiet eyes flick flames in his direction.

"Merena said that I would be released when you had gotten her pregnant."

Rainek leaned down so he could better see into her eyes. "That was her demand but I convinced her otherwise." He pulled her forward, nodding to Bren to release her. "Even if I wanted to sleep with Merena—" The fire exploded behind her lashes. He shook his head quickly to add strength to his words. "Which I don't. At all. But even if I did, I couldn't. Denith and I want only you."

She considered him for a long time then leaned forward. "Is that true, Denith?" she asked, looking deep into his eyes.

Rainek felt the dragon's presence cover his like a web of fine silk. He could watch but had no control. *Want only you. Have only you.*

The veil cleared seconds later and Rainek was back in charge. Lorran placed her hand on Tiana's wrist.

"Trust him, my dear. Biologically, you have the most faithful husband around."

Tiana glanced at Lorran then back to Rainek.

"Tiana, this is my mother, Lorran."

Tiana gasped. "I just flamed you in front of your mother?"

He chuckled and wrapped his arm around her waist, pulling her against his body. Denith shivered with pleasure at her warm, seductive scent. Rainek tried to ignore the hardening of his cock.

"Don't worry. She'll love you anyway." He nodded toward Bren. "You've met Bren. He stopped you from setting the room on fire. Or the rest of it, anyway. That's my sister, Kayla and—" He led her forward. "Father, this is Tiana, my future wife and Denith's mate."

"I'm very pleased to meet you, young one. Welcome to our family."

She's pregnant.

Tiana heard the words inside her head where she had grown used to hearing Denith speak, but it wasn't Denith. It was a new voice. She glanced at the two other men. Was it possible they were dragons as well?

I know, Denith proudly answered.

With all the voices in her head, it took a moment for her to adjust to what the first dragon had said.

"I'm what?" She looked up at Rainek. His eyes were black as he stared down at her, then as if the sun was rising inside him, the darkness disappeared and the amber glow returned.

"You're carrying my child," he said softly. The quiet announcement echoed through the chamber.

They had only a moment before a screech shattered the stunned silence.

"You're pregnant *and* you're a fire witch?" Merena stormed off the dais and stalked toward them. Rainek kept Tiana close. He didn't want to hurt a woman but no one was going to harm Tiana again. "But you've always been powerless. That's why you're hidden away in this forsaken pile of rocks. How did you suddenly become the most powerful kind of witch in the land?"

Tiana pushed her shoulders back and smiled at her sister. "Power comes from passion."

Merena's face turned red. She whipped around and faced the queen. "She seduced my consort and now she carries the seed that is rightfully mine."

"Remember what I said, Princess," Rainek said in a quiet voice that only Tiana could overhear.

Merena opened her mouth then snapped it shut. Anger still lit her eyes but she stepped back. Tiana didn't take her eyes off her sister but did flick a quick glance toward Rainek. She was going to have to ask him what he'd talked to Merena about. What would cause her to back down so readily?

Queen Leika stepped forward. She inspected Tiana with a critical eye. Since she'd been banished to the Keep—it was too embarrassing for the queen to have a powerless daughter— Queen Leika had ignored her. Now, there was a greedy twinkle in her eye as she stared at her middle child. "How long have you had your powers?" she asked.

"A few days."

"And you're already very strong." She hummed softly. "This is a wonderful development."

"I don't understand. Fire witches are feared and hated."

"Hated? I don't think so, but feared, yes." Queen Leika's eyes got big. "What a wonderful trait for a queen to possess." She looked at Rainek. "You think to marry the prince?"

The full reality of her power came back to Tiana and she shook her head. "No, Your Majesty."

"What?"

Rainek moved in front of her, blocking her from the queen's intense stare.

"Of course you're going to marry me."

"Rainek, I can't," she said, finally finding her voice.

"But you love me." He paused and she saw a moment of vulnerability. "Don't you?"

"Yes, but—"

"And you tolerated Denith well enough."

"I love Denith, but—"

The dragon's pleased rumble rattled the windows.

"Then there is no reason not to marry me."

"I'm a fire witch. Don't you realize what that means?" He obviously didn't. "Now that I've come into my powers..." She grimaced as she glanced around the room, scorch marks decorating the stone walls. "My hands always feel like fire. I burn whatever I touch. I'm a danger to everyone. Including you. I couldn't bear the thought of hurting you." She gasped. "Our child! I'll hurt our child."

Rainek shook his head. "Give me your hands." He held out his, palms up.

She drew away, crossing her wrists behind her back. The large body of his brother blocked her escape. In fact, his family seemed to form a circle around them. It was strange. Suddenly surrounded by three tall, muscled men, Tiana didn't feel the least bit nervous. They wouldn't hurt her. Unless she hurt Rainek.

"Come on, honey, trust me," he encouraged.

Fingers trembling and silently vowing to snatch her hands away at the first sign of pain, she stretched out to meet him, the heat from her palms blazing uncontrollably. She watched his eyes, and inched her fingers toward his. The tips of their fingers touched.

He didn't scream. In fact, he didn't even flinch. She smoothed her hand forward, feeling his palm slide beneath hers. The fire raged from her skin but he didn't seem to feel it. She lifted her hands free and stared at his. No redness, or singed flesh.

"How...?"

"I'm a dragon. We're creatures of fire." He took her hands back into his and smiled. "All I feel is warmth and passion. And love."

Tiana nodded, her heart melting as she stood there.

"And of course, you must marry him, my daughter. You carry his child." There was no mistaking the glee in Queen Leika's voice. When every eye in the room turned to her, she smiled. Tiana could see the pleasure in her eyes. She almost looked ready to clap her hands like a small child being given a present. "We'll celebrate the Joining now but when the child is born, we'll have a huge event with all the nations invited." The queen stepped forward and reached out to Tiana, being careful to place her hands on Tiana's shoulders. "The power of a fire witch and the strength of dragon blood. Can you imagine how powerful your daughters will be?"

A scream from beside the throne drew everyone's attention, just in time to see Merena plop down on the floor. "It's not fair. That was supposed to be my child."

Queen Leika rolled her eyes and shook her head. "I apologize for my youngest daughter. She's always been a bit spoiled. Now, if you'll excuse me, I'll call for wine and food and we'll plan the Joining Ceremony for tomorrow."

As Queen Leika walked away, Tiana found herself surrounded again by Rainek's family. This time his mother and sister joined them.

"Welcome to our family," Lorran announced, stepping forward. With a slight smile, she said, "You'll have to learn to control your temper because I really don't want my tapestries burned to cinders." Tiana blushed at the teasing reprimand but she nodded. "Don't worry, my dear. I'm sure as soon as you realize Rainek belongs to you alone there'll be no cause for tantrums like this one."

"No, Your Majesty."

"Please, call me Lorran. I'm so thrilled to meet you at last." She hooked her arm around Tiana's elbow and began to lead her away.

Rainek watched for a moment, before he realized his mother was expecting to have a long chat with his bride. Denith grumbled in his head.

"Uh, Mother, I need to steal Tiana away for a little while." Denith growled again. "A fairly long while, actually."

Lorran blinked, her eyes fluttering innocently as she stared at her middle son.

"Why?"

"Uh, it's been five days since Denith and I have...been near Tiana." He walked forward and took Tiana's hand in his, pulling her away from his mother. "We *really* need to spend some time alone."

Kei wrapped his arms around his wife's waist and pulled her against him. "You go on, son. Your mother understands."

Lorran laughed and put her head on Kei's chest. "After thirty-two years with a dragon, I suppose I do."

"Thank you." Rainek bowed quickly to his parents then grabbed Tiana's hand and ran out of the room.

"Perhaps we can find our chamber as well, my love," Kei whispered not so quietly into his wife's ear. With a teasing laugh, she took his hand and followed him out.

Kayla sighed as she watched her parents leave, then turned to her remaining brother.

"Looks like it's you and me," she said. It would be hours, if not tomorrow before they saw their parents or their brother again. "Unless you're going to go scouting for a mate amongst the witch women?" she asked.

His eyes turned flat. "No. I have no intention of accepting a mate the dragon chooses."

Kayla knew Bren's feelings on the subject and let it drop. "Want to go play chess?"

"Sounds fine." Together they turned and walked toward the door.

"Rainek did look happy though," she said, unable to keep the wistful tone out of her voice.

* * * * *

"You look happy," Tiana said, recognizing the same emotion in herself. Rainek had explained about Merena and her potions and spells. She could well believe it. It made so much sense and if Tiana knew if she hadn't been seeing the world through a broken heart, she would have recognized it as one of Merena's plots.

Tiana brushed the long strands of his hair away from Rainek's face and looked up at him.

"Why shouldn't I be happy?" he asked with a gentle smile. "I have you. Denith is content. We're going to have a child." He shifted, driving his hard cock the merest fraction farther into her. She sighed as a delicious spike of need moved through her pussy. "And did I mention...I have you?"

Tiana smiled at his teasing, trying to hide her doubt.

"What's wrong?" he asked, obviously seeing through her attempt.

"It's just this power of mine." She placed her hands on his back lightly, to reassure herself she wouldn't harm him. "It's increased by passion." She felt her cheeks warm. "If I stay with you, I'm going to set everything on fire. The furniture. My clothes. What about our child?"

As if he couldn't resist a little movement, he pulled his hips back and then thrust in, once again settling himself inside her.

"Our child will be part of each of us. I doubt fire will be able to hurt him." He grinned. "Actually, it will probably be a her won't it?"

Tiana smiled at the reminder that her people gave birth primarily to girls.

"And as for the house, we'll get metal furniture, and I'll help you dress. And undress." His face turned serious. The solid honesty in his eyes struck her again. When he looked at her like this, she knew he was speaking from the depths of his soul. "We will make it work because I can't be without you. I love you."

Tears pricked the edges of her eyes and started down her cheeks. As if the sight of her tears frightened him, Rainek hesitated. "Oh, honey, please don't cry. Please don't." He kissed the tears away and then trailed his mouth down her neck, nipping her skin as if to distract her. It worked. When she squirmed beneath him, he slowly began to thrust, sliding his cock in and out—not striving for a climax but simply moving inside her. She stroked her hands up his back, across his chest, loving the feel of his skin beneath her hands. She could touch him—finally touch him—as she desired.

They loved slow and long, letting the need build between them until it could no longer be contained between their two bodies and it burst from them.

She sighed with pleasure, feeling Rainek come inside her and then accepting his heavy weight on top of her as he collapsed down. He stayed in that position, nuzzling her neck until Tiana realized he'd fallen asleep.

She wrapped her hands around his back and held him to her.

"Mine," she whispered.

Enjoy this excerpt from
Just One Night
© Copyright Tielle St. Clare 2003

Chapter 1

"It's the least you could do."

Geneva Bryce almost ignored her sister's whine but knew it wouldn't stop there.

"No," Geneva corrected. "The least I could do is nothing. Which is what I'm going to do." She signed the requisition form and placed it on the stack of outgoing mail. As always, her desk was tidy and organized. The only disruptive force was Jessie.

"But you owe me," Jessie insisted.

Geneva lowered her pen and looked over the top of her glasses. "How do you figure that?"

"I covered for you the night you snuck out to lose your virginity."

Geneva's jaw dropped open. "That was thirteen years ago."

"Still, I covered for you and you never paid me back."

"I helped you graduate from college."

Jessie shrugged. "I guess, but this is *really* important."

The wheedling tone in Jessie's voice ground on Geneva's already strained nerves. *If I give in now, the whining might stay at a tolerable level.*

"I don't understand how this is going to help," she said shaking her head.

"Wilson's brother hates me." Jessie's lower lip curled into what Geneva supposed was an adorable pout. But after watching Jessie pout for twenty-two years, it was no longer adorable. Geneva raised her eyebrows in silent question. "His brother thinks I'm a bimbo."

And where would he get that idea? Geneva kept that comment to herself.

"So, Wilson says we can't go out anymore." Fat, fake tears pooled in Jessie's eyes. "You just have to help me."

Geneva sighed. "What do I have to do?"

Jessie's tears disappeared as quickly as they'd formed. Not a single one had escaped. No reason to risk the mascara. "It's simple. You'll go on a date with Wilson and meet his brother. After Bradford—"

"Wilson and Bradford? Who would torture children like that?"

"They're family names. Anyway, you act like a complete bimbo, and then when Bradford sees how dumb you are, I'll seem perfectly fine to him and he'll give Wilson his blessing."

Geneva shook her head as her sister's words finally penetrated. "You want me to act like a ditz so that you'll seem normal?"

"Exactly."

Geneva couldn't resist glancing at the diplomas on her wall. The top one declared her Geneva Bryce, Ph.D.

"I'm not that good of an actress."

About the author:

Tielle (pronounced "teal") St. Clare has had life-long love of romance novels. She began reading romances in the 7th grade when she discovered Victoria Holt novels and began writing romances at the age of 16 (during Trigonometry, if the truth be told). During her senior year in high school, the class dressed up as what they would be in twenty years—Tielle dressed as a romance writer. When not writing romances, Tielle has worked in public relations and video production for the past 20 years. She moved to Alaska when she was seven years old in 1972 when her father was transferred with the military. Tielle believes romances should be hot and sexy with a great story and fun characters.

Tielle welcomes mail from readers. You can write to her c/o Ellora's Cave Publishing at 1337 Commerce Drive, Suite 13, Stow OH 44224.

Why an electronic book?

We live in the Information Age — an exciting time in the history of human civilization in which technology rules supreme and continues to progress in leaps and bounds every minute of every hour of every day. For a multitude of reasons, more and more avid literary fans are opting to purchase e-books instead of paperbacks. The question to those not yet initiated to the world of electronic reading is simply: *why?*

1. *Price.* An electronic title at Ellora's Cave Publishing runs anywhere from 40-75% less than the cover price of the <u>exact same title</u> in paperback format. Why? Cold mathematics. It is less expensive to publish an e-book than it is to publish a paperback, so the savings are passed along to the consumer.

2. *Space.* Running out of room to house your paperback books? That is one worry you will never have with electronic novels. For a low one-time cost, you can purchase a handheld computer designed specifically for e-reading purposes. Many e-readers are larger than the average handheld, giving you plenty of screen room. Better yet, hundreds of titles can be stored within your new library — a single microchip. (Please note that Ellora's Cave does not endorse any specific brands. You can check our website at www.ellorascave.com for customer recommendations we make available to new consumers.)

3. *Mobility.* Because your new library now consists of only a microchip, your entire cache of books can be taken with you wherever you go.

4. *Personal preferences are accounted for.* Are the words you are currently reading too small? Too large? Too…ANNOYING? Paperback books cannot be modified according to personal preferences, but e-books can.

5. *Innovation.* The way you read a book is not the only advancement the Information Age has gifted the literary community with. There is also the factor of what you can read. Ellora's Cave Publishing will be introducing a new line of interactive titles that are available in e-book format only.

6. *Instant gratification.* Is it the middle of the night and all the bookstores are closed? Are you tired of waiting days — sometimes weeks — for online and offline bookstores to ship the novels you bought? Ellora's Cave Publishing sells instantaneous downloads 24 hours a day, 7 days a week, 365 days a year. Our e-book delivery system is 100% automated, meaning your order is filled as soon as you pay for it.

Those are a few of the top reasons why electronic novels are displacing paperbacks for many an avid reader. As always, Ellora's Cave Publishing welcomes your questions and comments. We invite you to email us at service@ellorascave.com or write to us directly at: 1337 Commerce Drive, Suite 13, Stow OH 44224.

THE
ELLORA'S CAVE
LIBRARY

Stay up to date with Ellora's Cave Titles
in Print with our Quarterly Catalog.

TO RECIEVE A CATALOG,
SEND AN EMAIL WITH YOUR NAME
AND MAILING ADDRESS TO:

CATALOG@ELLORASCAVE.COM

OR SEND A LETTER OR POSTCARD
WITH YOUR MAILING ADDRESS TO:

CATALOG REQUEST
c/o ELLORA'S CAVE PUBLISHING, INC.
1337 COMMERCE DRIVE #13
STOW, OH 44224

Discover for yourself why readers can't get enough of the multiple award-winning publisher Ellora's Cave. Whether you prefer e-books or paperbacks, be sure to visit EC on the web at www.ellorascave.com for an erotic reading experience that will leave you breathless.

www.ellorascave.com